sweet control

SUGARED AND SPICED
BOOK 4

LADY MARIE

Cover design by Lady Marie

Editing by A.K. Edits

Formatting by SHON

contents

For the Sugared & Spiced girlies. Thank you for seeing this through to the end.

content warning

This book features a large age gap, adult language, sexually explicit content, kink specifically involving dominance and light bondage, adult parenting growing pains, father/daughter conflict, brief physical violence and sugar daddy/sugar baby relationships and dynamics.

Read with care and have fun!

philip

BEING a father wasn't exactly going the way I'd expected. That wasn't necessarily a bad thing. In fact, it was going pretty well, all things considered. I'd never intended on having any kids. Barely thought twice about it.

There wasn't a paternal bone in my body—at least I hadn't thought so. I mean, all in all, kids were fine. I wasn't a part of the "fuck them kids" movement or anything, but if I spent too much time around them, I tended to get a bit... squeamish. Hell, even when I was a kid, they made me uncomfortable. Maybe it was the way they seemed to see way too much, leaving me feeling exposed. Shit, maybe it was just how sticky they always seemed to be from all the candy they ate.

I didn't know. Either way, having one was never on my to-do list. At fifty-one years old, my plan was to live my life as an unattached, very attainable bachelor until either my heart gave out or my dick stopped working. Whichever came first.

And then Trinity showed up on my doorstep. Or

rather, showed up in my voicemail and then in my office. Thirty seconds with her and suddenly I couldn't imagine a life where I *wasn't* a dad. I didn't have any trouble believing who she said she was. She looked exactly like her mother, not one piece of me in or on her face, but there was still no denying she was mine. I knew it from the instant connection I felt with her. Someone different might have been upset about losing so much time with their daughter, but me? I just wanted to make up for the lost time. *Instantly.*

It was sort of unbelievable, honestly. Trinity was sweet, insightful, quiet, observant. Just about the opposite of me in every way. Except her laugh. When it came to her laugh, we were identical.

Trinity was also, unfortunately, ignoring me at the moment. I was quickly learning that parenting was all about trial and error. Wait, was it really parenting when the kid was already twenty-six years old? Any real parenting that needed to be done was long over, something she'd not so kindly reminded me over the phone earlier when I once again asked her when I was going to meet this mysterious boyfriend of hers.

Every time I brought him up, she changed the subject. With the way her entire face lit up whenever they were on the phone or texting one another, it was obvious he made her happy, so I couldn't figure out what the problem was. Which one of us was she hiding, him or me? Maybe it was a bit of both.

The one saving grace was the last time I'd spoken to her mother, she said she hadn't met him yet either. That gave me at least a little comfort. Still, with us both living in Oakwood now, I'd hoped she'd want to include me in more of her life.

Apparently, my mistake was saying that to her instead of keeping that thought to myself.

"Fucking dramatic as always."

I swear she sounded just like her mother when she said those words. And it wasn't like she was wrong because okay, maybe I was being just a tad bit dramatic. Trinity wasn't shutting me out of her life completely, just in that one little area. We still met multiple times a week, spending plenty of quality time together, but something about the way she tightened up whenever I mentioned her new relationship just didn't sit right with me. I mean, she'd only been here a few months. How fast were her and this guy moving? How did she even meet him? *Where* did she meet him, for Christ's sake?

I'd tried asking her all of those things a few weeks ago, when I'd first heard about him, but I couldn't get anything out of her. Trinity kept her answers short and sweet. She'd gone out to a party with her best friend and she and the mystery man connected there. When I asked what party, she didn't answer. After trying to sneak in a few more questions, she'd shut the conversation down entirely.

You would think I would've learned my lesson then, but I'd always been hardheaded. That's why she wasn't answering any of my calls or text messages now. Yesterday I called myself "putting my foot down," *demanding* to meet this boy to see what he was all about and if he was worth her time.

Want to know what else she'd apparently gotten from her mother?

Her temper and ability to cuss a person out so thoroughly that they damn near needed a change of underwear once she was done. I hadn't even been able to register the lack of sound on the other end of the line after she'd hung up. I swear it took me almost ten minutes to actually pull the phone away from my ear and then another five to try calling her back. Okay, so maybe that's an exaggeration, but you get the point. My not-so-baby girl had me shaking in my boots and I wasn't afraid to admit it.

As I made my way through the entrance of Honey and Ivy's hotel bar, half of me wanting to check to see how things were going on this Friday night and the other half just needing a drink, I tried calling her number one more time.

"Trinity, I'm sorry," I said to her voicemail, leaning against the bar. "Please just call me back. I promise I'll drop the whole thing and won't ask any more questions." *Liar*. "Just...I just want to know if we're still on for our movies and mimosas date on Sunday."

Over the last three months, we'd made a habit of meeting for movies and brunch every Sunday. I cleared my schedule, no matter what it was someone else wanted me to do, just so that day could be reserved for the two of us. It was the highlight of my week even though our taste in movies tended to be very different and neither one of us made it halfway through them without complaining about the other's selection.

Ending the call, I gave a sigh as Bryant, one of the bartenders, set my standard choice of two fingers of scotch in front of me. A vibration in my hand drew my attention just as I picked up the glass.

TRINITY:

I'll see you on Sunday.

Okay, so she couldn't be too upset with me if she was keeping our date. My lips curved in a smile, ready for my first sip of scotch, when a voice broke into my thoughts, halting my movements.

"Looks like TLC aren't the only ones who ain't too proud to beg."

The smoky voice was right next to me and as my eyes lifted to find the owner, I realized I had to have been more distracted than I thought. That was the only explanation for why I hadn't noticed a literal goddess.

My eyes scanned her from head to foot, taking in her honey-colored skin, pretty white toes, curvy frame, and gorgeous heart-shaped face accented with a small nose ring. She may have been seated, but even from this angle, the way the slinky black off-the-shoulder dress dipped low, showing an almost obscene amount of cleavage, and clung to the curves of her body both made me weak in the knees and struck me directly in the chest.

"Does all that gray on top of your head mean you don't hear as well as you used to, or are you thinking about how grateful you are you won't have to sleep on the couch when you get home tonight?" She snickered while sipping her martini.

My mouth finally caught up with the rest of me as I slid her a smile. "Oh, I heard you just fine considering there's not nearly as much gray up there as you're trying to imply." Little did she know, I'd started to go gray a lot earlier than fifty-one and long ago found a barber who knew how to color my hair in a way that left just enough silver to make me look distinguished, but not old. "I was just a bit distracted by the most beautiful eavesdropper I've ever met."

Instead of swooning like I'd hoped she would do, she scoffed, angling her body away from me, which only made me move in a bit closer. Not close enough to make her uncomfortable—at least I hoped not—but enough to hopefully keep her attention.

"I'm pretty sure whoever had you begging and pleading just now wouldn't appreciate you flirting with me. That'll definitely get your ass put back on the couch. It would be a shame for all your hard work to go to waste." This time, instead of a scoff, she rolled her eyes to let me know how unimpressed she was.

"Mmm...first off, I've never been made to sleep on a couch a day in my life." I'd spent a few nights on the couch in my real estate development office over the years, even on my couch here in my office at the hotel, but that was by choice, not necessity.

"And second, I don't think my daughter really cares who I flirt with." My eyes traced along her body one more time. "Though your interest in who I was on the phone with is noted. Don't worry, gorgeous, I am very much unattached."

She gave me her own once-over before responding. "Now that you mention it, talking to your daughter does make a bit more sense. Sort of lends itself to the whole 'man way beyond his prime who just can't let go of his youth' thing you have going on. Doesn't exactly mesh well with the idea that you're the type of man who'd fall to his knees for a woman over voicemail."

Damn. She clearly not only thought she had me all figured out but was enjoying taking shots at me. Any man with a bit of common sense would've probably been offended, but me? I was actually enjoying this. Did that mean I had more than a bit of common sense or none at all?

"Believe me when I say I've dropped to my knees plenty of times for a woman's benefit. And I've never minded one bit."

A small fire lit behind her eyes, disappearing so quickly I almost thought I imagined it.

"I'm sure." Her tone screamed she wasn't interested, as did her body language, but I wouldn't be me if I didn't give it one more try.

"I'm Philip."

"And I didn't ask."

"Is that because you really don't care to know or because you're having such a good time torturing me?"

"Neither." She brought her eyes back to mine as she finished off her drink and I felt another presence walk up beside me. "It's because getting to know you, whoever you are, just isn't on my agenda for the night. Getting to know *him* is."

I turned in time to see a man with an uncertain smile on his face standing right next to me. Funny how she joked about my age, but there couldn't be that big of an age difference between me and her date.

"Sorry I'm so late. I got caught at the office," he said, looking uneasily in my direction before refocusing on her. "Would you like one more drink before we head to dinner?"

"I think one was enough to hold me over."

"Okay, I'll just settle your tab and—"

I cut him off before he could finish. "No need. It's taken care of." A quick nod in Bryant's direction as he cleaned up her glass made it clear I would handle it.

"Okay, well...I suppose we can head out then," her date said, still unsure. She slipped her jacket on as we took each other in. The fact that he hadn't protested my declaration let me know what sort of man he was right off the bat. I doubted if he could even handle a woman with the type of fire this one clearly had, but I kept my thoughts to myself. She'd find out on her own soon enough.

"Enjoy your evening," I said, a smirk playing on my lips as she moved past me.

Instead of responding, she returned my smirk with one of her own before placing her arm in his and heading toward the door. I didn't know how and I didn't know when, but I knew for sure we'd be seeing each other again.

I couldn't wait.

TWO

NOPE.

Next.

Hell no.

Absolutely not.

I rolled my eyes as I pushed away from my desk and stood, ready for another glass of pinot. Finding the type of man I wanted should not be this difficult. Wasn't dealing with a website like *Sugared and Spiced* supposed to take all of the hard work out of dating?

Okay, so this wasn't exactly "traditional dating," but that's what made the shit even more frustrating. A sugar daddy was supposed to be the non-complicated way for me to get exactly what I wanted, but so far, all I've managed to meet were fucking boring ass duds.

Technically, they weren't all duds.

No. I was not about to be worried about some random ass man at a bar. I didn't even know why he came to mind. It wasn't like I'd met him on the site.

No, but he was the most interesting part of the night.

Not like it was hard when you compared him to Malcolm.

I let out a snort as I took the few steps necessary to get to my kitchen. I needed some extra butter popcorn immediately. Might as well make that while I top off my glass.

On paper, Malcolm had been promising. He was fine as hell, well-established in the marketing world, and hadn't even blinked at the monthly allowance requirement on my profile. Honestly, even the conversation between the two of us at the restaurant the night before hadn't been horrible. It was our first time out together and he was obviously nervous, but I'd hoped as the night went on, he would loosen up and get a bit more comfortable. Instead, it was like the longer we sat there, the more his ass clammed up.

Part of me enjoyed it. I always loved a challenge and he seemed like just the type of man who could benefit from my particular brand of...relief. I smirked at the thought of having him on his knees, one red bottom pump pressed into his chest as I made him kiss along the edge. Would he melt into the floor? Would his body relax? Would he whimper or groan as he gave control over to me?

As each question entered my mind, so did the picture of a different man on his knees for me. One that stood at least five foot nine to my five-seven, with skin just slightly darker than my own. A man whose hair was just long enough to see the gray peppered throughout both it and his mustache and dimples he knew all too well drew women in. The man from Honey and Ivy to be exact.

Thinking about it, that cockiness of his might be a lot more fun to play with. Especially since something told me as much as Malcolm might want or need for someone to help him give up control and unwind, it was far-fetched he'd actually be up for trying it. And as much as the financial piece of a sugar relationship was important to me, sex was equally high on my list. There was no way in hell I was going to sit in a relationship, even one with a sugar daddy, if my sexual needs weren't being met. I was not going to sacrifice a toe-curling, body-shaking orgasm just for a few coins.

A girl had to have standards.

Speaking of a body-shaking orgasm... Maybe that's what I needed to clear my head. Right now it was all lackluster dates and unappealing profiles. That's not what I wanted to be thinking about. No, right now, I wanted an empty head and a throbbing pussy. And I knew just how to get both.

Abandoning my original mission for popcorn, I grabbed my newly full wine glass and headed toward my room, silently throwing up thanks I'd had the foresight to charge my favorite vibrator before heading to yoga this morning.

Shoutout to Saturday morning Raegyn for being a horny bitch.

I couldn't help but laugh at my own thoughts. Grabbing the dark purple rose toy, I sipped more wine as I headed into the bathroom, turning on my shower. While I usually liked to have my water on hell, I took it down a few notches because the last thing I wanted to do was burn my skin off while trying to find my release. It didn't take long to strip down and take two more gulps before slipping into the already steam-filled glass area.

I started slowly, leaning against the wall, not caring about my hair or the cool tile against my skin. My right hand drifted like it had a mind of its own, grabbing one full, heavy breast before my fingers rolled across the already hardened nipple. The electricity that shot through me was immediate. My nipples had always been one of the most sensitive areas on my body and right now, I used that to my advantage, each twist and pull making my pussy thump.

With my eyes closed, my other hand went searching for what was between my legs, finding it sticky and dripping, the wetness having nothing to do with the water from the showerhead.

"*Oooh* fuck." The words spilled out on a moan as my back arched and I cupped my breast again, this time lifting it just enough to allow my tongue to dart out across the hardened bud.

My breath caught in my throat as I started to ride my hand, fingers parting my lips just enough to touch my swollen clit before putting the toy exactly where I wanted it.

It didn't take long to conjure the picture I wanted in my head. There he was, on his knees at the bottom of the bed, eyes staring up at me as if begging for my approval like he'd just finished making me come with his tongue. The vision sent shivers through my body. Or maybe that was the combination of vibration and suction around my clit. Either way, I couldn't help the whimper that escaped. Even in my fantasy, it was obvious he wasn't used to the shift in power dynamic and *fuck*, I think that turned me on even more. Those eyes, which had been filled with mischief and defiance last night, were lit with heat and desire now.

"Fuck me," I gasped, the order escaping naturally. Honestly, I wasn't sure if the words were just in my head or I'd said them out loud.

It didn't matter.

He crawled up my body, not questioning my directions at all. It happened so fast. One minute imaginary Philip was crouched over me and the next, that dick of his, the one I just *knew* was thick and heavy even without having seen it, was pushing into me at a speed so slow it felt like fucking torture.

As I turned, pressing my forehead to the cool tile, I could feel him. It didn't matter that he wasn't actually here with me. I could feel each thrust forward and each reversal back. Shit, I was pretty damn sure I could even feel the way his breath caressed my skin as he whimpered into my neck and that...that was what really did it. The imaginary sound and picture of him reduced to nothing but whimpers as my walls gripped and pulsed around him sent me spiraling toward my orgasm.

Screams filled the shower as my knees buckled and my hand slapped against the wall in an attempt to keep myself upright, even as I never moved the rose from my clit. My thighs shook as my juices spilled out of me, mixing with the water swirling toward the drain.

"Shit, Philip. I—*shiiit*," I whined as I squeezed my eyes tighter, not ready to let the vision or sensation go just yet.

And then the scene changed. Now it was me who was on their knees as I practically unhinged my jaw to take him between my lips. Even with this new position, the power I felt didn't change as I pictured myself damn near sucking his soul out of his dick.

"Please, Miss Raegyn."

His begging sounded so real. Maybe he really was in the room with me. It was hard to tell the difference between this fantasy and reality, especially with the blood pounding in my ears and the moans falling from my lips. The desperate way he said my name sent me right back over the cliff as my moans sounded off even louder than they did the first time.

Holy shit. My chest heaved, my thighs had a delicious ache, and my clit was so sensitive that even after snatching the rose away, it still felt like it had its own heartbeat thanks to the aftershocks.

It'd been a long time since I'd come that hard, that much, and that fast. I had to take a few minutes to catch my breath, but once I did, I tossed the toy to the side and took one step on shaky legs, then two, to grab my wash cloth and clean myself up.

Not having the strength to wash my now soaking wet hair, I made a mental note to just do a quick co-wash in the morning before finishing up, turning off the water, and wrapping an extra long bath sheet around myself.

My entire body was spent. Wrung the fuck out, really. I hadn't intended to go so hard, but as I grinned at my reflection, ready to go through the rest of my bedtime routine, I didn't regret it one bit. Especially since I knew the chances of me actually getting to experience that sort of fun with him were slim to none.

But still...a girl could dream, right?

philip

"I'M GOING TO KILL YOU." The words came from the pit of my stomach and I meant every one.

"Philip..." a familiar voice behind me warned, but I didn't bother shooting the owner a second glance.

"No, you can't save him this time, Benji. Arthur has officially gone too damn far. He crossed a line and you damn well know it."

Here I thought I could trust my friend only to have him betray me in one of the wildest ways possible. I couldn't believe this shit. When I invited my three best friends to the hotel to catch up, I'd been prepared to maybe corner Arthur and pump him full of alcohol so he'd finally share some information about his new girlfriend. But this... I hadn't been prepared for this.

"You're being dramatic." By the tone of his voice, it was obvious how annoyed Benji was with me, but I didn't care. My outrage was justified and we both knew it. They all knew it.

"Are you really surprised? Philip is a drama king if I've ever seen one. Why are we all acting like this is our first time meeting the man?" Seth said with a snort as he took a seat in our usual rounded booth. I typically made sure it was left reserved for moments just like this one. Well, maybe not *exactly* like this one, but for times when any or all of us wanted to get together.

"Fuck you, Seth. I am not being dramatic." *Well... maybe just a bit.* "Arthur lost my favorite *and* most expensive pair of cufflinks! And if that weren't enough, he had the nerve to lose them at a hotel that doesn't belong to me!" It was fucking egregious. The cufflinks could be replaced, but giving money away to my competition? Did Arthur have no sense of loyalty?!

"Well..." I said, eyes glued to his face as he settled into the seat across from me. Benji slid in just before I did, him and Seth both letting out matching heavy sighs confirming they were over my antics. Too bad.

"Well what?" Arthur said, taking a sip of his drink. He clearly thought this was a joke.

"What do you have to say for yourself?"

His eyes traveled to Seth, then Benji, which I assumed was him looking for a bit of help. "Ummm...I'll replace the cufflinks?"

"Fuck the cufflinks! Why would you take your girl-friend to The Valantis instead of bringing her here? Espe-cially since you could've gotten a suite here for free."

"Now you're just lying through your damn teeth, you pompous asshole," chuckled Benji. "When was the last time you gave any of us something for free?"

"Free, heavily discounted. Same fucking thing." They wanted to play semantics while I was trying to get some damn answers. "And why do you keep jumping in like Arthur needs saving? He's a grown ass man. He can speak for himself. Unless your girlfriend's got you on a short leash now." I sent a smirk in Arthur's direction.

Was it me or did the man look...nervous? Looking around to see if I was the only one who noticed it, I froze right before bringing my tumbler of scotch to my lips.

"Wait...have y'all already met her?" Their immediate silence was answer enough. "I don't believe this! What are you, ashamed of me or somethin— *Don't fucking say it.*" That last part was for Seth, who had already opened his mouth to answer.

"Relax, Philip. Nobody's ashamed of you."

"Speak for yourself, Artie boy," Benji snickered. I flipped him off and focused back on Arthur.

"It...just hasn't been the right time to introduce you. That's all."

"Well, why not?" As much as I liked to give my friends a hard time and...well...get on their last nerve, the fact that I seemed to be the odd man out on this one was actually bothering me. I mean sure, maybe I joked a bit too much, drank a little more than I probably should, and talked a whole lot of shit, but there were actual feelings buried beneath all that. I would've thought my friends knew that about me. Looks like I was wrong.

"What's the problem? Does she have an extra toe or something? Wait... I haven't dated her, have I?" The words were meant to alleviate some of the tension at the table and maybe deflect from the hurt in my voice just a few moments ago, but it was Seth choking on his drink that broke the ice.

"Christ, Seth, get it together. I was only joking." Seriously, what the fuck was wrong with everyone today?

"Nothing like that, I swear," Arthur said, passing Seth a napkin and patting him on the back. "It's just...complicated."

"Okay, well, un-complicate it."

As I waited for him to do just that, I took a look around the bar so I wouldn't have to watch as he came up with his next excuse. I preferred not to be upset with my friends if I could help it. Instead, I wound up doing something better: laying eyes on the gorgeous woman who'd been the star of my dreams for the last week. As if she could feel my gaze, she turned and locked eyes with me.

"On second thought, I'll let you off easy. For now." I didn't even stop to see what, if anything, they thought about my sudden change of heart. "Next time we talk, though, I expect a full explanation on how and when you're going to introduce me to your mystery woman. And why you saved the best for last."

I made quick work of sliding out of the booth, leaving them to figure out...whatever the hell it was they needed to figure out. There was something more important that deserved my attention. Or rather, *someone* more important.

For the last week, a certain gorgeous woman had invaded every one of my free moments—and some not so free if I was being honest. Not knowing her name hadn't stopped me from wondering how her so-called "date" had gone.

Did he talk too much? Was he too quiet? Had he dragged his fingers along the curve of her thigh the way I'd wanted to while I watched them—*her*—walk away? At the end of the night, once she'd been fed and taken care of, maybe even thoroughly entertained, did she let him give her a chaste kiss before she slipped into her car and headed home or had she given him a bit more?

Christ. Why did the thought of his lips on her in any capacity piss me off so bad? I couldn't remember the last time a woman had me this off-kilter. Shit, had any woman ever had me feeling like this?

Pushing the question out of my mind, I focused on making it across the room before my favorite ball of fire decided to disappear on me. Again.

No sooner had I walked up behind her did she let out a laugh. "You know stalking is actually illegal, right?"

A smirk appeared on my face as I leaned forward, putting myself just inside her line of sight. "Well, if that's the case, maybe I should be the one to call the police. I mean, this is my hotel after all."

Based on the raised eyebrow and the look on her face, it was obvious that was new information for her. "Now, when they ask me the name of the woman who can't seem to stop herself from following me around, what should I tell them?"

I didn't expect her to answer me, so when she did answer, it did something to me.

"You can tell them Raegyn just couldn't seem to stay away."

"Raegyn, huh? Gorgeous name for a gorgeous woman."

That earned me both a snort and an eye roll. "Are your functions automatically set to lay the bullshit on thick, or is it just a habit you're having a hard time trying to break?"

"Depends. Do you always give the men interested in you a hard time or is that just reserved for me?" I shot back without missing a step.

"Oh, trust me, you are not that special."

She finally turned to give me her full attention and the way her eyes traced over every inch of me sent the type of thrill through me I didn't even know existed.

"I'm not sure you're special at all, honestly," she continued. "But I'll admit you're not too bad to look at. That works in your favor."

A compliment wrapped in an insult? Be still my beating fucking heart.

"And I guess you're going to tell me whoever your date is for the night is miles ahead of me in both areas."

It looked like she was contemplating how to answer the question as she toyed with the olive in her martini glass. "Fortunately for you, he was even worse off in the special department than you are. So it looks like I'm entertaining myself for the rest of the night."

"That's one option."

The way she pulled her bottom lip between her teeth had all the blood rushing from my head down to my dick. And damn if the head tilt she sent my way didn't make it clear she knew exactly what she was doing.

"And what's the other?"

"That you spend the evening with me." It wasn't too late, just about ten at night, which was why I'd assumed she was waiting for a date, not just fresh off of one. There was plenty of time left in the night for us to get to know one another.

"I'm sure you're used to that being a tempting offer, but I'll pass, Philip."

As unaffected as she wanted me to believe she was, I must've left some sort of impression if she'd remembered my name. There wasn't much time for me to dwell on it, though, since she was already grabbing her small clutch and sliding off her stool. Without even a second glance at Bryant because...well, let's face it, we both knew I was going to cover her tab again, she quickly made her way toward the exit in the direction of the lobby. I didn't even think about it, just ran after her, probably looking every bit of a fool. Ask me if I cared.

Raegyn was out of the bar and halfway down the hall before I finally caught up with her, reaching out to lightly grab her wrist and praying she didn't reach back and slap the shit out of me.

"Now hold on there, Miss Raegyn." Was it just me or had the name caused something to flash in her eyes?

Heat?

Desire?

Whatever it was, I wanted more. "You're not even going to give me a chance to plead my case?"

"I hadn't planned on it."

"Well, that's not exactly fair now, is it?"

She slid her wrist out of my hold but didn't quite pull away like I'd expected. "Trust me, Philip," she said as she used a finger to trace small lines up and down the inside of my forearm, her path growing longer each time. Surprise, surprise, that wasn't the only thing growing. The hard dick I *thought* I had before was nothing compared to the goddamn steel in my pants now. "I don't think you're ready for my particular brand of fun."

She leaned against the wall, pulling me with her, and I followed right along, a more than willing participant. I leaned toward her, taking in her jasmine and orange blossom scent, and a noise rose from my chest that I didn't quite recognize. Was that a growl? This fucking woman had me growling and we'd barely touched each other.

"Sounds to me like you're making a pretty snap judgment." My eyes focused on hers and it took everything for me not to break the contact. *Fuck*, it was hard. Those fingers of hers were trailing along my arm again and that leg, the one on full display thanks to the jaw-dropping purple cocktail dress she wore, was pressed against my thigh as if she were daring me to get even closer.

You don't have to tell me twice.

"Maybe, but it seems to me like you're the sort of man who enjoys being in control."

She wasn't wrong, I did, but right now? Right now I felt more out of control than a runaway train. "You say that like it's a bad thing."

"Oh, it is. At least for me." She beckoned me closer and I gave in, only stopping when her lips grazed my ear. "Because when I'm with a man, Miss Raegyn is the one in charge."

The words tickled my ear, but there was nothing funny about this feeling. Not when one of her hands was suddenly cupping me through my slacks.

Christ. My next words were tumbling out of my mouth without a second thought. I didn't know where the hell this road would lead me, but I was down for the ride. Down *bad* as the kids said these days.

"Show me."

FOUR

THIS WAS NOT the original plan. When I found myself back at the Honey and Ivy hotel bar after another lackluster *Sugared and Spiced* date, I told myself it wasn't because I was hoping to see *him* again. Definitely wasn't because I was hoping he'd be there looking to get another glimpse of me, and I swear it wasn't because every time I'd drenched my fingers in cum for the past week, it was with his face in my head and his name on my lips.

That's what I told myself, but as soon as he appeared in front of me, I had to stop bullshitting. It was all a lie. The way I wanted this man should've been a sin. My desire was building like a slow burn, moving from the tip of my toes up through my thighs and straight through my goddamn pussy.

This was...wild. How was I even considering giving him what he was asking for when, let's be real, what did I even know about him?

His name? *Check.*

The fact that he owned a gorgeous hotel and probably had deep pockets, one of my favorite qualities? *Check.*

Don't play. You know at least one other thing.

Okay, yeah, I did. If the look he was giving me was any indication, I knew Philip wanted me just as much as I wanted him. Maybe even more. *Check and mate.*

My words had clearly made him curious. Curious about what it was like to give up the control we both knew he walked through life wielding. He couldn't deny the shit was tempting, even if it would just be for a little while. So instead of giving him a playful smirk and heading home by myself, I listened to the tiny voice in my head telling me to let Philip take me somewhere with enough privacy for me to give him exactly what he'd asked for.

We didn't touch as we made our way to his private elevator and then down the secluded hallway that led to his office. We didn't need to. It was like we were both confident the other wasn't going to change their mind. Like we just *knew.* And maybe we did.

"Should I be nervous that your office is so far away from everything else?" I asked once we'd made it and he closed the door behind us. I took in the room. It was...gorgeous. My eyes scanned across gray walls with built-in shelves, each adorned with one thing or another but still somehow not appearing cluttered. From there they took in the deep cherrywood desk, which I realized could pass for the twin of my dining room table if it weren't for the three tall ivory wingback chairs that surrounded it and the matching plush couch not too far from the door. They were almost out of place considering the set was probably made for a living room, but as one of my favorite singers once said, almost doesn't count. They fit the office perfectly. Fit him perfectly.

"Not at all. I just happen to like my privacy."

"If you say so." I smirked. "Persian?"

Without asking, he already knew I was referring to the rug I was so sure would feel like pure heaven if I slipped off my red bottoms and ran my toes through it.

"Of course."

I couldn't help but laugh at the cockiness in his voice. Even his stance, the way he leaned back against the door, arms crossed in front of his chest and head tipped slightly forward, just radiated big dick energy. And he knew it.

"So how exactly does this work, Miss Raegyn?" The way he said the moniker wasn't serious, but it still did something to me. Why else would I be clenching my thighs together for dear life?

"Well, first off, that's exactly how you'll refer to me while we're in scene."

"Scene?"

I nodded. "That's typically what it's called when you slip into this sort of space or activity. Like two actors taking on roles in a play, except what we're doing here is very, very real."

"Okay," he said slowly as he took in my words. "And our roles would be..."

"Dominant and submissive." I gestured to myself and then him respectively. "Do you need me to explain what exactly that means?"

"I'm somewhat familiar, but explain what it means for you specifically. Like you said...I'm used to being the one who runs the show."

I couldn't help but smirk. Instead of standing still, I moved slowly through the office, checking out the pictures in frames and the trinkets he'd most likely picked up while traveling.

"In simple terms? It means you giving control over to me...willingly. You wouldn't do anything you're not comfortable with, but I'd be taking charge. Sometimes that looks like giving you tasks that focus on what makes me feel good, and sometimes...sometimes it looks like me taking satisfaction in overwhelming you and your senses with your own sexual pleasure."

"And both of those situations turn you on."

I came to a stop in front of his desk and looked him in the eye. "Yes because either way, they both make me feel powerful. I'm the one deciding what's happening and you're trusting me enough to know when it comes down to it, I'll take care of us both. Trusting me to unlock something in you that may be unfamiliar but will give us both the exact pleasure we're looking for, whether you know what that looks like or not."

He didn't respond right away. Was he taking everything I'd said and really considering it or trying to come up with a way to tell me to get the fuck out?

"That's probably a lot to ask right? For you to trust me when you don't know shit about me."

"Probably, but I'll admit I'm still intrigued. Show me." He gave me a small smile. "Please."

There were those two words again. On their own, they were powerful, but when coupled with the word *please*, they sent a shiver running through my body.

Over the years, I'd taken the time to try multiple things and discover what exactly turned me on. Everything wasn't for everybody. I enjoyed inflicting a bit of humiliation, but not to the point it made my partner cry. Just a little...embarrassed. Impact play was another fun one, though I never used anything harder than my cute semi-soft flogger or matching crop. I wasn't sure he was ready for that type of thing yet, but if we ever got the opportunity to go there, I just knew his caramel complexion would redden up perfectly. Since we were starting from the beginning and this was a bit more impromptu than either of us originally anticipated, tonight we'd keep it simple and just see if he could follow a few directions.

Instead of using words, I crooked my finger at him, instructing him to come toward me. Rubbing his thumb across his bottom lip, he didn't give the command a second thought, immediately following through. I knew exactly what he was going to do before he even did it. He moved to encircle me but stopped as I pressed a hand against his chest.

"You're not in charge here, Philip. Remember? Unless you've changed your mind."

I watched as his eyes caressed every inch of my body. It was like I could literally feel his hands on me even though he'd dropped them to his sides. His hooded gaze told me how much he wanted to touch me. How much he was contemplating giving me just a bit of pushback. Wondering how I'd react if he took those hands, currently opening and closing into fists, and touched me anyway.

He was easy to read simply because those were the same thoughts that went through every man's mind whenever I explained to them my particular brand of kink. Just because his mouth said he could be into this didn't mean he wouldn't go to war with his brain about whether or not that's true. I had no delusions that Phillip knew one hundred percent what he was getting himself into. That was part of the reason I wanted to take this slow and start out simple. Show him what it meant when I said he wasn't in charge. By the end of the night, he'd be getting the taste of me he wanted. He'd just be getting it the way *I* wanted him to.

His eyes flashed with desire and something else. Just a hint of defiance. "No, I haven't changed my mind."

"Okay. In that case, we need a safeword."

He tilted his head. "Exactly how wild do you plan to get in this office, Raegyn?"

Hmm... I'd let it slide for now since we hadn't actually started yet. "Not too wild, I promise. But it's always important to have one just in case...for both of us."

He nodded in understanding. "Is there one you typically use?"

"There is."

"So let's go with that. I'd rather use something you're more practiced with."

"Okay." I leaned back, making myself comfortable on the edge of his desk. "Tweety."

"Tweety? That's your safeword?" He shot me an amused look.

With a giggle, I nodded. "Yep. It's silly, but trust me, it's effective since it's not something you'd usually hear during sex."

He chuckled as he rolled his eyes and loosened his tie a bit. "Tweety it is, then."

"Okay, Philip...on your knees." It wasn't a request, and the way my tone changed left no room for debate or questions. Playful Raegyn was gone and Miss Raegyn was her replacement.

He hesitated. It was just for a second, but I caught it before he put his game face on and gave me a small nod.

My eyes tracked each movement as he dropped to the ground slowly, first on one knee and then the other. The way his eyes never left mine had my insides doing flips worthy of a professional gymnast. How was it I had all the power here, but the intensity behind his gaze almost made me want to reverse our roles? *Almost.*

"Good boy." The words were practically a purr and I immediately noticed the vibration it sent through his entire body. Did my little cocky hotel connoisseur have a praise kink? I made sure to file that away for later. "Who knew you could take direction so well?"

"Clearly not you," he said, a smug smirk on his face as he sat back on his heels, trying to shake off the way the words made him feel. It was easy to see what he was doing and why, but that didn't mean I would be letting him get away with it.

"I don't remember saying you could speak to me. Especially not in that smart ass tone." The sound of my acrylic nails tapping against his desk filled the brief silence. "But don't worry, we'll find a much better use for that mouth of yours."

My eyebrow arched, almost like I was challenging him to respond. To be fair, I was. Even though I craved his compliance, a part of me wanted him to push back. Brats were their own type of fun, especially when it was your job to tame them. Luckily for me, Philip didn't disappoint.

"I think I like the sound of that." He leaned forward ready to touch me again, almost like he was impatient to get started. What he didn't seem to understand, though, was that we'd already started. Or maybe he did and he was just testing my limits. Either way, I was going to enjoy helping him learn tonight's lesson.

"That's strike number two." My voice hardened and his eyes shot away from my thighs back up to my face. "You're way too eager to touch me. Maybe I shouldn't let you since you seem to be so hardheaded."

"Bu—" he started, but the look I sent his way made him think better of whatever he'd been about to say.

"Let's have a little lesson on who's running things, shall we?" As beautiful as he looked on his knees, for this I was going to need him in a different position.

"Have a seat." I gestured toward the plush chair I'd moved to the side during our conversation and he stood, ready to do exactly as I asked. "But first..." My eyes darted to his belt. "Drop 'em. Now."

After taking about thirty seconds to figure out what I was referring to, his hands made slow work of undoing his belt and pants. The sound the buckle made as it hit the floor seemed to echo in my ears. Or maybe that was my heartbeat flooding my senses. My adrenaline always seemed to shoot up whenever I was in scene.

I waited for him to take a seat and watched as he made an attempt to move the chair closer, but I stopped him, placing a heel-clad foot against the edge of the seat cushion between his thighs to keep it in place. "No, you're fine just where you are. Take him out."

This time he knew exactly what I meant as he lifted just enough to slip himself out of his designer briefs.

Fuck.

Philip's dick was just as beautiful as I'd imagined. It wasn't extremely long, but that didn't matter. What he didn't have in length, he sure as fuck made up for in girth. He had to be holding the thickest, prettiest dick I'd ever seen, and the way the tip glistened with his precum even though we had barely gotten started? Yeah, maybe we should skip right to the part where I climbed in his lap and bounced on it until his cum coated my walls. My pussy clearly liked the thought as she clenched around empty air.

No, not tonight. Maybe next time. If there is a next time.

Who was I kidding? There was absolutely going to be a next time. I already knew it.

"I want you to stroke him for me. Can you do that?" My tone was smooth as silk. "Take those strong hands and your thick, perfect dick and show me what you looked like while you thought about me this week."

"But Miss Raegyn," he said, and because he slipped into character so beautifully, I let him talk out of turn. "Who says I thought about you this week?"

Toying with one of the tight coils that had fallen in front of my face, I leaned forward just a touch. "Are you going to lie to me and tell me you didn't? Because if you do, I might just have to consider that strike three."

He shook his head almost instantly, so fast I couldn't help the giggle that escaped.

"Exactly. So be a good boy and do what I said. Let me see what it looked like when you thought about me while you were in the shower...and wrapped up in your expensive sheets...and when you were right here in this office, sitting at this desk, supposed to be hard at work."

He didn't have to tell me which scenario I'd gotten right because I knew it was all of them. We were both way too drawn to each other for me to be the only one to make myself come at the thought of us this week. I'd spent the last seven days crafting my own visual, but I wanted something real to hold onto. Something I could think about when I went home tonight and made myself come right after he did.

This may not have been what I had in mind when I started the night, but I certainly couldn't be mad at where this was headed.

philip

THE LAST TIME I sat in this office with my dick in my hand, I was behind my desk as I pictured Raegyn wearing the same black dress she'd had on when I first laid eyes on her, trying to find some type of fucking relief so I could get even just five minutes of work done. Now here I was, three days later—same office, same dick, different chair, with the goddess herself sitting in front of me, telling me to do the exact thing I'd been doing then.

And they say dreams don't come true.

My heart felt like it was going to beat right out of my chest. It hadn't even been that long in this—what had she called it? A scene?

We'd barely even started, but from the moment her tone changed, something in me snapped to attention. I thought it was simply the sexual tension between us, and then she issued those two words.

"Good boy."

Never in my life had anyone said some shit like that to me, and if you'd told me even a few days ago a woman would, I would've told you to keep them away from me, but now... Now I wanted nothing more than to hear her say those words again. It was like it satisfied an unknown itch in the back of my brain.

"Are you going to make me repeat myself?" she asked, snapping me out of my thoughts. Her foot tilted forward a bit, putting the slightest amount of pressure on my thigh, making me groan.

"*Fuck*," I hissed, not because it hurt but because it was turning me the fuck on. When she said she'd be running this show, she'd really meant it. Confidence and power were practically pouring off of her. This was her element and she looked goddamn good in it.

She lifted her foot so that I could slide my briefs off completely. As they hit the floor, I made note of the wet spot right in front. My eyes flicked down to my dick taking in the precum already dripping from my tip.

"Not you making a mess for me already, Philip," she giggled. "If I thought you deserved it, I might suggest I use my mouth to clean that up for you. Maybe next time." My gaze snapped up to meet hers because damn it, I wanted it. I wanted that shit real bad.

I tightened my grip around the tip of my dick and more precum appeared as I fought back another groan. Using it to coat my hand, I began to stroke myself just as she requested—no, demanded—making sure to twist my wrist whenever I hit the top of my shaft, just the way I liked it.

Between the intensity of her gaze and the bolts of electricity shooting through me as I fucked into my hand over and over again, my eyes fluttered shut and my pace quickened, already chasing my release.

"Aht-aht, did I tell you to speed up, baby?"

Her voice sounded husky, and the thought that

watching me was turning her on? Fuck, why did that make me want to go harder?

"Let me see you take your time. We're not in a rush, are we?"

Shit, maybe she wasn't, but I'd never wanted to come so bad in my fucking life. I was desperate for it.

"I'm not ready for this to be over yet." The way she said those words sounded like it came out as a moan. Was it? "I'm having too much fun watching you fuck that beautiful dick of yours with your hand. *Too fucking beautiful.*"

That was abso-fucking-lutely a moan.

"Go slow, baby. Can you do that for me?" She was asking, but we both knew just like her first set of directions, it wasn't a request.

Even still, I found myself answering, "Yes, Miss Raegyn," as I opened my eyes. The smile that spread across her lips made me feel as though I was on top of the world. Or maybe that feeling was coming from the tight grip and slow stroke I was currently giving my dick.

Okay, so the latter definitely played a part, but I was confident that knowing I'd pleased her was the main culprit. This was...uncharted territory for me.

When I'd told Raegyn to take the lead and show me what she liked, I hadn't imagined it would affect me like this. Despite the fact I was leaning back in the chair, trying to pace myself as my hips began to slowly thrust forward to meet my hand, it felt like I was on the edge of my seat. The anticipation was killing me.

What was she going to say next? Was she enjoying the show? Were my groans turning her on? Or maybe it was the way my chest heaved that was doing it for her. Fuck, I was pretty sure my eyes were beginning to glaze over as that ball of pleasure started to build in the pit of my stomach, growing inch by inch as I felt a familiar warm tingle in my balls. I could barely see straight, but I could still feel the heat of her gaze on me and couldn't help but wonder if that's what made her enjoy this so much. The knowledge she hadn't even let me touch her yet, let alone touched me, and somehow she had me seconds from falling apart. It had to be written all over my face as I wrinkled my brow in concentration.

"You look ready to come. Is that true? Are you ready to make a mess all over your hand for me? The t-type of mess that'll have me on my knees ready to clean you u-up?"

Every so often, she tripped over her words. I didn't understand why because...shit, I couldn't see her. When the fuck had my eyes closed again?

"Christ, y-yes," I hissed out.

"Yes, who?"

I forced my eyes open and the sight in front of me almost had me spilling every drop of cum I had.

At some point from her position on my desk—and fuck me if I knew when—Raegyn had moved her foot from the edge of my chair and propped it up onto the other one. With her dress hiked up at the hips and her thighs spread apart, she looked like pure sin. One hand was cupping her sex while the other gripped her exposed breast. Clearly I'd been oblivious to just about everything around me while in my trance. *When the fuck had she pulled her dress down?*

I couldn't even ask because just then, her tongue snaked out, flicking against her nipple before she sucked it into her mouth and caused my brain to short-circuit.

"Shit!" I hissed out as my balls began to tighten up.

"Don't even think about it!" Raegyn barked out, and my spine immediately snapped straight as my hand stuttered to a stop.

Between the heavy breathing and heady feeling, I could barely get my next words out. "Bu-but—"

"You don't come until I tell you to, do you understand?" My head did something that barely resembled a nod. "And when you do make that beautiful dick of yours come, it'll be because you made me come first. Do you understand *that* too?"

I wanted to say no. I wanted to say fuck that and stroke my dick until the balls-deep feeling hit me again, but I didn't do either. Instead, all I could do was nod as my blood roared in my ears and my dick pulsed in my hand.

"Good," she said with a gasp, and it was then I realized she wasn't just cupping her pussy. She was playing with it. "Now be a good boy and get over here so you can make Miss Raegyn come all over your tongue."

There wasn't an ounce of hesitation in my movements as I clumsily scrambled to do as she said, making her giggle. She could laugh all she wanted, but I was confident about one thing. Despite the fact she quite literally had me by the balls, once my tongue took the first swipe across her slit, laughing would be the last thing on her mind.

"Are you always this eager?" she gasped out as I nibbled on the inside of her thigh before immediately dipping my tongue into her pussy. Fuck, she tasted amazing. Both sticky and sweet, with a slight delicious hint of something I couldn't describe. If they bottled this up and sold it in stores, I'd buy out the inventory every opportunity I got.

"Only when I know I have a Michelin star-worthy meal sitting in front of me." I grinned as I used two fingers to push her lips apart. Her already swollen clit peeked out and I could hear it begging for my attention.

"Mmm, are you just going to look at this pretty pussy

or are you going to be on your best behavior and give it a kiss?"

Instead of using my words, I wrapped my tongue around her clit, sucking it into my mouth. The wail she let out was music to my ears and I opened my eyes in time to see her tossing her head back as she used both hands to grip the edge of my desk. It was the only leverage she had as she lifted her hips, pushing her pussy into my face for more.

I loved it here. Eating pussy was one of my favorite pastimes, but eating Raegyn's pussy was by far one of the best things I'd ever done with my life. If I died right here, right now, between her thighs, tongue deep in her treasure, I'd die the happiest fucking man on earth because *this* was my idea of heaven.

With each alternating movement between her clit and her pussy, she rolled her hips, the threat of her orgasm looming over both of us. I needed to taste her cum. I went into overdrive, my silent way of begging for what I wanted. Well... maybe not so silent since with each taste, I groaned with appreciation.

Fucking paradise, and I meant that shit.

"So goddamn good," she whined, and even though at this point her thighs were like my own custom pair of earmuffs, I heard her loud and clear. Her next words came through crystal clear as well.

"Stroke it for me, baby. Spill that cum all over your hand while I bless your tongue with mine."

Finally.

The satisfied groan I let out had to have sent vibrations through her entire body. With one hand still between her thighs, slipping two fingers into her warm walls, my other hand went straight to my dick so I could do exactly as she told me.

My tongue stroked along her swollen clit as I fucked both of us. The dull tingle in my balls sharpened as they tightened, the cliff I'd been running toward earlier coming at me full force. If anyone walked in right at this moment, they'd get a fucking eyeful, but I didn't care. The combination of her juices on my tongue, the way her pussy clamped around my fingers as she called out my name repeatedly, and the visual of what we must've looked like sent me falling over as I pulled away. Her inner thighs were covered in her cum, but it didn't faze me as I pressed my forehead against her skin there, curses flying out of me as jets of warm cum shot out of my tip and landed all over my hand and expensive ass rug.

I must have blacked out because I could barely catch my breath as the world around me slowly came back into focus. My fingers were still on autopilot, pushing into her as the aftermath of her orgasm sent tremors through her body. Her own fingers were lightly running through my hair as her whispers filled the room.

"Look at what you did, Philip. Are you proud of yourself? Because you should be, baby. You did so well."

At the sound of her words, I nestled my cheek against her skin, taking in her delicious smell as what she said settled over me, calming my spirit. What type of fucking witch was she and what sort of spell was I under?

"Give me your fingers."

I slipped them out of her pussy and held them up, watching as she leaned forward to taste the flavor her cum left on them. I was spent, yet the sensation of her tongue between my fingers made my dick twitch like it was attempting to come back to life.

"Now let me taste you too."

There was a twinkle in her eye as the words slipped

from her lips. Pulling the first hand back, I lifted the other and watched as she cleaned each finger one by one. A whimper—an actual fucking *whimper*—left my chest.

"Maybe next time, I'll let you taste it too."

Fuck, this woman was going to be the goddamn death of me.

SIX

"MISS MA'AM, YOU DID WHAT WHERE?!"

I damn near choked on my cranberry mimosa as multiple eyes in the restaurant turned in our direction.

"If you don't lower your damn voice," I giggled. "Fucking around with you, they're gonna put our Black asses out of here." Our food hadn't even come yet and I'd been dreaming about the oxtail from this restaurant all damn week.

"I wish they would, as much money as we spend up in here on a regular basis." Kali kissed her teeth as she took a sip of her own drink. She made a good point. We were at Jerk Dynasty at least three times a month and that didn't even include the takeout orders we placed on a regular. Why learn to cook when the chef here could do it for me and be ten times better?

I'd say it was ridiculous if their food wasn't so damn good, especially their Sunday brunch. Endless mimosas and small plates of various Jamaican and American dishes.

Somebody could judge us if they wanted to, but they'd just have to kiss my ass and judge they mama first.

"And anyway, stop trying to change the subject and get back to telling me about you and this nasty ass hotel aficionado of yours." A mischievous smirk crossed her lips as I rolled my eyes.

"He's not *mine*," I stressed.

"Hmph, could've fooled me. If you can get a man who doesn't belong to you to do all of *that* in his office during business hours, I can't imagine what type of shit you could pull once you claim him."

With a raised eyebrow, I asked, "First of all, since when is ten at night considered 'business hours'? And second, who said I wanted to claim him? Maybe I was just bored and needed a little fun after that dry ass date I had."

As the waiter came with our first bit of food, Kali scoffed. Knowing my best friend of six years was knowing she was about to not only fuck this food up, but do it while clocking me since we both knew what I'd just said was a load of bullshit.

"First of all, as you so eloquently put it, that man owns a hotel. All hours are business hours for real. And second, I'm screaming at the fact you think you finna play me like I don't know you just as well as you know yourself. Girl, you have to be feeling him if y'all did all that."

"How you figure?" I wasn't trying to imply she was wrong, but I wasn't about to admit she was right either.

"'Cause I know you, friend. You don't share that side of you with just anyone, mainly because men tend to get fucking weird like you're challenging their manhood or something. Hell, that's half the reason you haven't found someone on that damn site you actually like."

I narrowed my eyes at her as I got ready to dig into the

braised oxtail and grits in front of me. "And your point is?" As soon as the food hit my tongue, I couldn't stop myself from moaning and shaking my head. "Too fucking good, I swear."

"And I swear if Philip had you sounding anything like that the other day, you'll definitely be seeing him again. You like the man, so don't even deny it. *That*, friend, is my point."

"Kali, I barely *know* him."

She shrugged. "An irrelevant point. You're getting to know him in the best way possible. Enjoy it and don't think about it too hard."

Kali dug into her chicken and waffles, leaving me to both my thoughts and my food.

Despite my weak ass protests, I knew she was right. I may not have known a lot about Philip, may not have had a profile to list out all his qualities or even had a real date with him, but what I did know was the fun I'd had with him the other night had been...fucking amazing.

To be honest, I'd been expecting him to freak out a bit after the scene ended. Shit like that could be overwhelming, especially the first time, so it would've been understandable if he needed some space. Instead, he let me clean him up in the private bathroom in his office and didn't even blink when I explained the concept of aftercare to him.

The intensity of what we'd done had adrenaline pumping through both of us, so it was second nature for me to have him sit down and take a breath to come down from the high. I smirked as I remembered how he'd insisted on sitting in his desk chair while we waited for one of his employees to bring us a late-night snack to replenish our energy.

"If we sit on the couch, what excuse will I have to get you in my lap?"

"Really, Philip?" I'd said, rolling my eyes as my hands fell to my hips. "If this is your way of trying to get me to fuck you tonight, it's not happening."

"Trust me when I say it certainly crossed my mind, but no, that's not what this is about. You've exhausted me, gorgeous, so I don't know if fucking you would even be physically possible for me right now. Though if you told me that's what you wanted, I'd be willing to try."

"Hmm, we'll have to work on that stamina of yours, old man." Snickers fell from my lips as I grabbed a bottle of water from his mini fridge and then took my place on his lap. His hand came up in an attempt to take the bottle from me, but I slapped it away before he could. "Let me do it. Taking care of you is my job as your—I mean as a domme."

There wasn't much room for him to argue, not when I was already taking the cap off the bottle and holding it to his lips. As I urged him to drink with one hand, the other stroked the back of his neck slowly. Instead of fighting me, he did as I asked.

If the woman who came in thought the sight of us was strange—or if she noticed how disheveled we looked and the interesting...stain I'm sure was on the floor—she didn't say anything. Just set down two plates with something that smelled suspiciously like grilled cheese and fries, along with some fruit, and then headed right back out of the door.

When I questioned why a grilled cheese of all things, he just said, "Who doesn't love a gourmet grilled cheese?"

He had me there. No other explanation needed.

"And don't think I didn't catch that jab about me being old. Trust me, this old dog knows a few tricks."

"Ewww, you better not be over there imagining all the

This time when I pulled myself from my thoughts, it was for the waiter who had come to take our second order, not Kali, though she was giving me a knowing look. Having a best friend who could read you like a good book was a pain in the ass sometimes.

"Stop looking at me like that," I said, pushing a stray curl from in front of my face while trying not to blush. Before she could respond, my phone vibrated in my purse. I quickly reached for it, glad for the distraction. Turned out it wasn't too much of a distraction, considering the message was from the exact person invading my thoughts.

PHILIP:

I managed to go a full day without texting you. Is that a point for me or against me?

RAEGYN:

I haven't decided yet.

PHILIP:

What if I throw in the added note I only went that long so you wouldn't think I was desperate?

RAEGYN:

What if I said I like you better when you're desperate?

PHILIP:

Well, then I'll text you all day, every day, gorgeous. You ain't said nothing but a word

RAEGYN:

That's what I like to hear.

RAEGYN:

Tell me you miss me.

PHILIP:

I miss you so damn bad I can't think straight, Miss Raegyn.

"You are down *bad*, friend, and you don't even realize it." Kali snickered from the other side of the table as she finished off her drink.

Giving her a wink, I looked down to see another message had come through.

PHILIP:

What are you doing Wednesday?

My bestie was wrong about this one. I was definitely down bad, but I also *absolutely* knew it. I was just deciding not to fight against it.

SEVEN

philip

"EXPLAIN AGAIN why I had to tag along for this?"

I chuckled as the car dipped in and out of traffic while I drove toward our destination.

"You didn't *have* to be here. I wanted you here."

"Mhmm, okay, so *why* did you want me here?"

Taking my eyes off the road for just a moment, I fixed them directly on her face, extremely aware of the effect she had on me. It would've almost been worth the danger to never take my eyes off of her.

"Who wouldn't want a gorgeous woman by their side for a little extra time?"

I focused back on the road, but that didn't mean I couldn't feel her gaze burning a hole in the side of my face. She stared for so long, I couldn't help but eventually crack a smile.

"Too much?"

"I love flattery as much as the next woman, but let's be for real." She giggled, and the simple sound of it made my heart skip a beat. That couldn't be a good thing. At least not while I was in the middle of operating heavy machinery. Weren't there laws against that sort of thing?

"I am being real. We had a date planned for tonight, but I didn't want to wait all day to see you, so...here we are."

"Mhmm...and where exactly is here?"

"The car. You have been in a car before, right, gorgeous?"

Despite the fact I wasn't looking at her, I still managed to dodge the smack she sent my way. Well, not completely, but getting hit in the shoulder as opposed to the back of my head was a win in my book.

"You are such a smart ass and absolutely full of it," she huffed, but even I could tell there was no real aggravation to her words.

At any rate, I was actually telling the truth; I did want to spend extra time with her.

We'd been talking non-stop for the last few days, whether it be texting, phone calls, or FaceTime, and somehow, I still couldn't get enough of her. Even the fact I had actual work on my plate didn't seem to deter me. I still found myself checking in with her just to hear her voice or see what she was doing.

My hotel practically ran itself, with the very valuable help of my on-site manager and staff, of course. There was still plenty of business I needed to handle, though. Some items just required my special touch. The problem was, I didn't want to give Honey and Ivy that touch...

I only wanted to give it to Raegyn.

"Be serious for two seconds, please."

"Fine," I said with a small chuckle. "I need to stop by my friend Arthur's place. He's been dodging my calls, but he can't ignore me if I'm standing at his front door."

"This isn't about those cufflinks, is it?"

"No, I promise." Honestly, I'd forgotten all about the cufflinks and the fact I'd told her about them. "There are a few contracts I want him to take a look at for me. Since he won't come to me, I figure dropping them off is the next best thing." I paused before clearing my throat. "And... maybe I want to introduce you two."

I could feel the blush rising in my skin because quite frankly, I was not supposed to admit that to her.

It's not like my friends had never been introduced to the women I spent time with, but Raegan was the first woman in a long time I was excited about them meeting. And yeah, part of me wanted their opinion.

Had I known her long? No.

But that's why this felt like a good idea. Arthur was probably the most level headed out of all of us, so if he co-signed what I saw in Raegyn, then maybe I wasn't truly losing it by rushing into whatever this was.

"You're adorable, you know that?"

I narrowed my eyes as we pulled onto Arthur's street, heading toward his driveway.

"I'm not adorable. I'm incredibly rugged and masculine."

"Who says you can't be all three?" She leaned over, placing a trail of kisses from my cheek to my neck, sending shivers down my spine and blood rushing toward my dick.

How disgusted would my best friend be if I let Raegyn climb on top of me right here in front of his house and I just...slid it in?

What if it was just the tip?

Surely he'd understand.

Right?

"Come on here, nasty. I can already tell what you're thinking and I'm going to need you to stop thinking it. Save whatever it is you're visualizing right now for our date, please and thank you."

"Fine."

With a sigh, I turned off the car and climbed out. Any possible doubt in my mind about whether or not Arthur was here, which I hadn't even considered until right at that moment, was gone as soon as I saw his car in its usual space near the garage.

Perfect.

Three minutes later, I was starting to doubt myself since he still hadn't answered the door when it finally opened.

"Philip, what are you doing here?"

The smile that'd been on his face not even fifteen seconds before was gone, replaced by one a lot less enthusiastic. In fact...it looked like he was in pain.

"Damn, you could at least pretend to be happy to see me," I joked before turning to Raegyn, who was staring at us with an amused smirk on her face. "Gorgeous, this is Arthur, one of my oldest friends. Arthur, this is Raegyn, the love of my life and the most beautiful woman I've ever met."

Raegyn narrowed her eyes. "I know we've established this already, but you are *so full of shit*." After kissing her teeth, she turned to Arthur. "It's nice to meet you, Arthur. Don't listen to him, I'm just his date for the evening."

"That's what you think," I said in a low voice, but I knew she'd heard.

She could take me for a joke if she wanted to. If I had my way, this thing we were doing was going to extend long past today.

"Are you sure y'all are friends, PJ? He looks too innocent to put up with your shit. Then again, maybe that's why he looks so irritated. He knows all about your brand of shenanigans."

"I can't believe you just used the word 'shenanigans,' gorgeous. I thought I was the old dog here, not you," I chuckled, pulling her body into mine.

"Shut up," she said, leaning away from me, but her words were more of a giggle than an actual command. Good enough for me.

The sound of a throat clearing grabbed both our attention.

"Again, Philip, what are you doing here?"

Arthur checked over his shoulder before taking another step out the door, attempting to close it behind him.

"Well, you haven't been answering my calls since I saw you the other day, so I figured that meant you wanted me to drop by. You were supposed to look at these contracts, remember?" I held the folder up in my hand to give him a visual.

"So instead of just waiting for me to get back to you, you decided to just pop up?" He shook his head after giving a weak chuckle. "Typical."

With a raised eyebrow, he added, "Sure you want to put up with his ass? Might be more trouble than it's worth."

Obviously, that was for Raegyn, who just shrugged. "So far, it's not too bad."

"Ha ha, very funny, you two. Are y'all finished?" I took a step toward Arthur, ready to head into the house, but he stopped me.

"Seriously, Philip, you should've called first. I'm kind of in the middle of something." To emphasize his point, he placed his hand on the door frame. "I'll just take the folder and you can get back to showing this beautiful woman who's definitely out of your league a good time."

"Sounds perfect to me," Raegyn agreed.

Her words barely registered as the wheels began to turn in the back of my mind. As many times as I'd popped up over here, Arthur had never been this determined to keep me out of his house.

"What's the deal, Artie boy? You got company or something?"

"Would it matter if I did? Maybe I'm just trying to get some rest. It's been a busy couple of days for me."

He was trying to seem unfazed by my question, but I knew him better than that. Arthur was flustered, which meant he had to be hiding something. It was obvious he did *not* want me anywhere near the inside of his house. That could only mean one thing.

"She's here, isn't she?"

"Who?"

The words flew out of both Arthur and Raegyn's mouths at the same time and luckily, my answer was the same no matter who I was responding to.

"Your new girlfriend. The one you've been hiding from me. She's somewhere in there, which is why you're acting so cagey."

"I do—"

Before he could fix his lips to finish the lie, I was pushing past him into the house. Was this an invasion of privacy? Maybe, but if best friends couldn't invade your privacy, then who could?

"I can't believe you were going to keep hiding her from me, Artie! Come on, don't you think it's time to introduce me already? I showed you mine, why can't you show me yours?"

"Now why does it feel like I should be slightly offended?" Raegyn folded her arms across her chest as she followed behind me.

Okay, maybe not the best choice of words. "I just meant—"

"I know what you meant, and luckily for you, I'm in a good mood. You'll get a pass...this time," she assured me, bringing a smile to my face.

"Great. Now that we've got that figured out..."

Deciding I needed to move quickly before Arthur got over his shock at my audacity, I gave her a quick kiss and then made my way through the foyer to the kitchen, where I could hear music and the sounds of someone moving around.

"I've got to say, it's about damn ti—"

"Who was at the door, ba—"

Our sentences collided with one another, each stopping the other immediately.

No.

Hell no.

This was a sick fucking joke, right?

There was no way that was who I thought it was standing in the middle of my best friend's kitchen in nothing but a goddamn button-up. *His* goddamn button-up.

"Trinity, what the *fuck* are you doing here?"

philip

"DAD!"

The squeak in her voice as that one word slipped out only confirmed this nightmare was my actual fucking reality.

Funny how hearing her say that word over the last few months had filled me with joy, hope, and hell, more happiness than I could have ever imagined. But here—now—hearing it only made me feel sick.

How could one word be so...jarring?

I shook my head back and forth as if it would get rid of her voice, but it obviously wouldn't get rid of the vision right in front of me.

Fuck, I needed a drink. *But first...*

Pulling myself to the present, I realized everyone was just content to ignore me. Or maybe they were hoping my body would go into shock and I'd just act like none of this was happening.

If only.

"Maybe I'm trippin', but I'm pretty sure I just asked a

goddamn question yet no one is giving me an answer, so let me try this again. What the *fuck* is going on here?" I looked around, bewildered. "What exactly am I looking at right now?"

And please, God, let it not be what I think it is.

It didn't even register that I'd taken a step—or maybe three—in their direction until something tried to yank me back. No, not something, *someone.* A quick glance told me it was the pressure from Raegyn's grip that stopped me.

It took everything in me not to shake her off.

God, what was I thinking bringing her here?

"I'm fine," was all I said, hoping she would let go.

She gave me a skeptical look. "You're not fine, you're literally yelling."

Was I? I hadn't even realized it. Oh well.

"Of course, I'm yelling! No one wants to answer my fucking question!" I snapped.

"Calm down, Philip," Arthur cut in, moving next to her. "You're scaring the shit out of Trinity right now."

It was safe to say his words had the exact opposite effect of what his calm tone was attempting to do. Now, instead of just barely holding it together, I was seeing nothing but red as I looked at the two of them in front of me. Whatever small amount of restraint I had before was completely gone as I broke Raegyn's hold and my fist connected with Arthur's jaw.

I was vaguely aware of the words "Jesus, dad!" flying in my direction as Arthur took the force of my hit. The small amount of satisfaction I felt seeing him on the floor unfortunately did nothing to dull my anger.

"Calm down? Calm down?! My daughter is standing in your kitchen, wearing nothing but your *goddamn shirt* after doing God knows what, and you're telling me to calm the fuck down?!"

In that moment, the sound of my voice even scared the shit out of me. Before then, the word "roared" never actually made sense to me. Not when it was applied to people.

What were we, lions?

But now...now I understood completely. I'd never raised my voice or made a sound like that before in my life, but there was a first time for everything, right?

"Now, I'll say it one more time. Someone—anyone— explain to me what it is I'm seeing right now. Explain it like I'm a fucking fifth grader, please, and don't leave out the good parts."

Instead of pulling himself up, Arthur stayed right where he was on the floor and leaned back against the kitchen island. Probably for the best because I swear to God if his ass tried to get up, I was just going to punch him again, and this time, I couldn't guarantee I was going to stop.

"Trinity and I...have been seeing each other."

"We've been dating," Trinity corrected as she bent down to his level. "And I love him."

A wave of nausea hit me as I watched her reach out to gingerly take hold of his chin and get a look at the bruise quickly forming on his jaw.

"I'm fine," he whispered to her with a weak smile. "And I love you too, pretty girl."

"Give me a fucking break!" What, did they forget I was standing right in front of them? "You're joking, right? Please tell me you're not serious."

There was no way this was really happening.

"They seem pretty damn serious to me," Raegyn stage-whispered next to me. The minute my glare was turned on her, she threw her hands up in defense. "I mean, you asked. I'm just stating the obvious."

"If this is your idea of helping, stop," I said through clenched teeth.

She made a zipper motion over her lips and took a seat in a nearby chair. There wasn't even the least bit of concern on her face. Not one ounce of the panic I was experiencing, but why would there be? Raegyn had nothing at stake here. Shit, I'd probably be ready to pull up a chair and request some popcorn too, if it weren't for the fact that this was my damn best friend and daughter we were dealing with.

Kill me now. Or at the very least, let me start the fucking day over.

Confused wasn't even the word. "How did this even happen?"

"What do you mean?" Trinity asked, her voice soft and face slightly embarrassed.

I let out a low chuckle. "What do I mean?" The words came out just above a whisper, so I couldn't be sure if any of them heard me, but it didn't matter. "I mean how do you even know each other because I sure as hell didn't introduce you."

I shook my head as another thought came to mind. "Because silly me, I was under the impression you were dating the woman you met at the—"

It was the sheepish look they both gave me that stopped me in my tracks.

"Fuck me! This is the woman you met at the play party? The one from Masquerade Night?"

Their silence made the answer pretty damn clear, but I wanted them to say it. *Needed* them to say it. Admit it to my fucking face, even if all the pieces were starting to come together. I mean hell, it was suddenly so obvious.

The secrecy.

The way they both seemed to close up whenever I mentioned meeting whoever they were dating.

The nervous looks Benji, Seth, and Arthur were all sending each other when we met for drinks over the weekend.

Every one of them had known, yet no one had the decency to tell me. That realization pissed me off, but it hurt more than anything. Nobody thought I had a right to know? This was how I had to fucking find out?

Just the thought they were all having a good laugh at my ignorance set my nerves on edge. Why else would they all keep this from me if for no other reason than they thought of me as a complete goddamn joke?

I was spiraling and I knew it, but there was no way to shut my brain off to stop it.

Jumping back into the situation at hand, I snapped again. "Answer me, Arthur! Is my daughter the woman you've been fucking for the last few months?"

Standing quicker than I would have thought possible, he yelled, "Don't say it like that!"

Clearly, I'd pissed him off. He could join the club.

"Say it like what? Like that's what you've been doing? I mean, it's a fact, right? It's what you two are sitting up here telling me, isn't it? That you've been sleeping with my daughter. Oh no, wait, that's not it 'cause by the looks of things, there hasn't been much sleeping going on. It's that you supposedly *love* her."

The revulsion on his face at my words mirrored the exact same emotion in my voice.

Good.

"Dad, please, that's just...eww," Trinity groaned, face in her hands, and I couldn't help but laugh.

Did it sound as out of control as I felt right now?

"*Eww?* You think what I said was disgusting? No, what's disgusting is the fact *he's twice your goddamn age*, Trinity! What were you thinking?"

Her head snapped back, and in that moment, I wasn't looking at the sweet girl I'd come to know. No this was a woman who could pass for her mother's twin when she was pissed off. And it was clear she was *pissed the fuck off.*

"Hypocritical much, *Philip*?" she shot back at me. The way she emphasized my name made me flinch. Funny, I hadn't realized how much I'd gotten used to her calling me 'dad' until just then.

"What's that supposed to mean?"

"Hello!" Her words came out as a shout as she pointed to Raegyn, who didn't exactly look pleased to be back in the middle of what I'm sure was turning into her favorite show. "Pot, meet kettle! You're going to stand here and tell me she's older than me by more than a couple years? What, did you hire a personal assistant and just forget to tell everyone about her?"

Okay, so she had me there, but I wasn't about to admit it. Instead, the best I could come up with was, "That's completely different." Even I heard how weak the argument was.

"And how exactly do you figure?"

If I wasn't so distraught, the way she cocked both her hip and head to the side would have been hilarious. As it was, I was already trying to fight a smirk and stay indignant at the same time.

"Because we're both adults!"

"So are we!" She threw her arms up in exasperation.

"You've been a father for what, less than a few months, and suddenly you think that gives you license to tell me how to live my life? Newsflash, it doesn't."

The force of her words hit me so hard, I stumbled back as if she'd actually pushed me.

"So what, this is you working out your daddy issues? Great work. No, seriously, looks like you're doing a bang-up job." It was a low blow, and as soon as the words were out, I wished I could take them back.

"Fuck you, Philip!" Trinity took a step forward. "I came to Oakwood to get to know you, but if this is who you are, then clearly that was a mistake."

"You don't mean that," Arthur and I said at the same time. As if I needed his fucking help to talk to my own child.

But she's not a child. You missed out on those years a long time ago.

He stepped between us and faced Trinity. "He's just worried about you, that's all."

The way she seemed to melt in his arms struck me in the chest. I was taking blow after blow here today. How the fuck was I supposed to compete with this?

"Get your hands off of her."

I reached out to grab him, but instead, Arthur was turning and grabbing me, forcefully guiding me toward the exit.

"Don't push it, Philip. I'm trying to save your ass before you say something else you fucking regret."

"Oh, thanks," I scoffed, shoving him away from me. Favors were the last thing I needed from him right now. "This is bullshit, Arthur, and you know it. Otherwise, you wouldn't have been sneaking around, so please forgive me if I'm not ready to kiss your ass just yet."

"That's not—" He stopped, closing his eyes and taking a deep breath before starting again, this time in a softer tone. "That's not what I'm trying to do. You're right. We should've told you sooner, but let me be very clear about something, Philip."

After taking a few steps toward me to close the gap I'd created between us, he said, "I meant it when I said I love that woman in there. So what you need to know is if you don't get the fuck out *right now*, I will throw you out because I'll be damned if I let you hurt her just because you can't take your head out of your own ass."

What the fuck did he just say to me?

Before I could wrap my hands around his neck, Raegyn blocked my path. Where had she even come from?

"Alright, okay, listen," she started, looking between the two of us. "Emotions are high right now and everybody just needs to calm down."

"What I need is—"

"Shut up, Philip."

Her voice had slipped into the same commanding tone she used during our scene and instinctively, I listened.

Turning to him, she said, "Arthur, it was nice meeting you, but right now, you go back and take care of...Trinity." She said her name as if she was worried just hearing it would set me off again.

"And you," she said, turning to give me her attention. "You are going to head with me to the car so we can do as he said and get out of here. *Now.*"

Her tone didn't leave any room for argument and honestly, I wasn't sure if I even had the energy to fight back. While the anger and hurt still remained, the actual adrenaline I'd been feeling just a few moments ago left my body completely.

The walls were starting to close in on me. I needed to get as far away from this house and everyone standing in it as soon as possible.

"You're dead to me."

Without another word, I headed for the door, not even bothering to see if Raegyn was behind me.

NINE

IT'D BEEN two weeks since I'd been dropped off in front of my condo, listening to Philip apologize and ask for a rain check on our date in a distant voice that said he was here, but not really before speeding off like a bat out of hell.

Fourteen days with no texts, no phone calls, nothing. To be honest, it was throwing me off. Despite the fact that not too long ago, I hadn't even known this man existed, going from near-constant communication to radio silence was...disorienting, for lack of a better word. I didn't consider myself a needy person by any means, but Philip feeling not even a small urge to reach out to me was not on my bingo card.

Then again, I'm sure finding out his long-lost daughter was riding his best friend's dick from here to kingdom come right under Philip's nose wasn't on his either. Hell, if it'd been me? I would've crashed out, told everyone to go to hell and kiss my ass, in no particular order, and got the fuck out of Dodge.

Okay, so yeah, as far as excuses to ghost someone went,

that was a pretty damn good one. Top tier. A-plus, no notes.

No notes, that is, except the one I'd attached to the bouquet of flowers I'd sent him yesterday, telling him when to be at my place and that I wasn't going to take no for an answer.

Was I desperate?

No.

But when I found myself utterly bored with every man who came across my screen as I swiped through *Sugared and Spiced* since last seeing Philip, I knew something had to give. I wasn't just uninterested in their profiles but the thought of the men themselves. Each and every one of them fell flatter than they had before I met him, which I hadn't even thought was possible. That realization was what drove me to do something about it.

The fact that I missed this man was wild to me because I barely knew him, but that didn't change the facts. Guess that's just one more unexpected thing to mark off on my bingo board. I'd make sure to do that after Philip showed up.

If he showed up.

Oh, he's coming...and hopefully he won't be the only one. Actually...

Taking a look at my phone to check the time, I realized if Philip was coming then he should've been here by now. At the very least, he should've been close. Nerves ran through me as I resisted the urge to send him a message. He hadn't reached out to tell me he'd be here, instead opting to send a text thanking me for the flowers.

Again...I'd taken the time to send this man *flowers.*

Now, don't get it twisted. I wasn't one of those women who thought men couldn't get gifts, a bouquet, or anything else. As much as they got on my nerves, I wholeheartedly believed men deserved a little spoiling every now and then —as long as they were well-behaved. But the whole reason I'd gotten on that website in the first place was literally to find someone who would spoil *me*, not the other way around. And I hadn't even met him on the damn site.

Was this irony or just the universe being hilarious?

Still, it was apparently a moot point because it didn't stop me from putting on very expensive lingerie from one of my favorite stores or ordering food from the Italian bistro around the corner.

Nope, I did both of those things without giving them a second thought. Before I had a chance to regret it, my intercom was buzzing to let me know my special guest had finally arrived.

"I don't think I've ever gotten a bouquet of flowers before. Felt kind of nice."

The cockiness of the man leaning against my door frame should *not* have made me smile the way I did, but fuck it.

"You're late," was my response even though it was only seven minutes past the eight thirty deadline I'd given in my note. "And don't get too used to it." The words were teasing as I tilted my head to the side.

His eyes slid appreciatively over every inch of my body. Just like the last time he'd done it, I swore I could feel their touch on my skin.

Good to know it wasn't a one-off.

"Noted, and I'm sorry. Ran into a bit of traffic on the way."

He held up a small bag and I instantly recognized the name of a small but expensive as shit jewelry boutique near downtown Oakwood.

"What's that?"

"Something you can absolutely get used to. Assuming you forgive me for abandoning our date."

"You were already forgiven, but I'm not above bribes. Especially when they come wrapped in pretty packaging."

Eagerly plucking the bag right out of his hand, I turned and headed toward the bar counter separating my kitchen from my dining nook, fully aware his eyes were taking in the way my ass hung out of the lacy purple boy shorts.

Me, turn down a gift? Never.

I wasted no time pulling the nice-sized red box out of the bag. As soon as the top cracked open, a diamond-adorned Cuban link necklace captured my attention. It sparkled each time it caught the light and I couldn't help but gasp.

"How did you know?"

His face scrunched in confusion. "Know what?"

"That expensive jewelry makes my pussy wet?" I snickered.

He snorted and the little show of laughter brought a bigger smile to my face. Yes, I'd been trying to get him to laugh, but I was also very serious. Two birds, one stone.

"Call it a hunch."

He crossed the room, coming up behind me and holding out his hand. Understanding what he wanted, I handed him the chain and turned my back so he could put it on properly. The cool metal against my skin made me shiver before I gave an excited little dance and turned to face him.

"It's beautiful. Thank you."

His fingers reached out and skimmed the top of the necklace before dipping down to trace along the skin just under it and up along my collar bone. "You're worth it."

"Oh, there has never been any doubt about that, but I'm happy to know you're a fast learner."

He chuckled again, the new smile that graced his face even brighter than the last. With a shake of his head, he watched me for a moment as he rubbed the back of his neck. Was he nervous?

"I was serious about what I said at the door. I owe you an apology for what happened. That's not exactly how I imagined us spending our time together."

"And I was serious when I told you no apology was necessary. That day was...a lot. For everyone."

I had a few thoughts on that, but I knew better than to bring them up now. No, the first order of business was to keep his mind off of what happened and on something more productive.

Like me.

Or us, rather.

With that in mind, I made quick work of fixing us both drinks, a glass of my favorite wine for me and a tumbler of cognac for him since I didn't have the scotch I'd seen him drink before on hand. He didn't seem to mind as he sipped from the glass, giving it a nod of appreciation as his eyes roamed the kitchen, finally finding the food I'd set out on platters.

"Arancini, rigatoni alla vodka, eggplant Parmesan... what's this?" He walked toward the other counter and gestured toward two meat dishes, closing his eyes as he inhaled the fragrance wafting off of them.

"Veal Marsala and chicken cacciatore."

He raised an eyebrow at the array of dishes. I shrugged. "What can I say? I'm a woman who loves options."

"Only thing missing is—" He stopped mid-sentence

and shook his head as eyes caught sight of two other items. "Salad and garlic knots. Never mind."

"You really thought I'd have all this Italian food and not have salad and bread. Wow," I giggled.

"Well, obviously I stand corrected. You really cooked all this for me?" When Philip's eyes finally met mine, there was a glint in them.

Smirking, I took the few steps needed to stand directly in front of him, arms reaching up to wrap around his neck, pressing my body into his. From this angle, I already knew he had the perfect view of my cleavage. The hunger in his eyes and the way he reached down to grip my waist confirmed it.

"So cute you have so much faith in my opinion of you and my ability to cook," I snickered. "But definitely not. Cooking isn't really my area of expertise. I'm sure I could burn water if I tried hard enough." His hands moved down until they were cupping my ass and I swear my pussy purred.

"I did, however, put my mean ordering skills to work. Lucky for you, you get to benefit from my love of Italian food and tendency to overindulge."

There was a teasing quality to my words because while I did love both of those things, I'd also done this for his benefit.

"Amazing at ordering takeout? I can deal with that, especially since I'm equally as amazing at swiping my card for the same thing."

"I wonder what other *amazing* things we can do together."

"Hmmm..." Philip leaned down, tracing his nose along the nape of my neck, getting very deep into my personal space, not that I minded. With his breath ghosting along my skin the way it was, the only thing I wanted right now was to *feel* him.

Or rather feel even more of him because the hardness pressing against me made me clench my thighs in search of relief.

"Maybe we should find out."

Without giving me a chance to respond, he lifted me up, and I instinctively wrapped my legs around him.

There was no maybe about it. We were absolutely going to find out. Dinner would have to wait because right now, there was something else on the menu I wanted a lot more.

TEN

EVERY GROAN PHILIP let out as I nuzzled his neck, my teeth grazing his skin, sent a thrill of pleasure through me. He'd made the same noise with each step he'd taken toward my bedroom. Even once he'd stopped, right as he finally laid me on the bed and began to trace line after line down my body, I could still hear it. The sound was burned into my brain and the thought of it never going away... Yeah, I could live with that.

Even now, as I straddled him, inspecting my handiwork after wrapping both of his wrists together with a necktie and securing them above his head, I could practically hear those groans echoing in my mind.

"Too tight?"

"No." He said the word as calmly as possible, but there was still a slight tremor to it.

"PJ, if you're uncomfortable—"

"No, it's fine, gorgeous, I just... It's—"

"Different?" He nodded his head and I gave him a small smile. "Do you know why I chose this particular tie?"

As I asked the question, I leaned forward, trying to not

think about the fact that the movement pressed his hard dick, which was now only clothed in briefs, right between my folds. It took everything in me not to shift my hips again to recreate the sensation that went through me the first time. Instead, I focused on hovering my face over his as one hand pressed against his chest and the other gave the fabric securing his hands a light tug.

"It was the only thing you had on hand?" he teased, looking up at me.

My giggle couldn't be helped. "No. Because when I saw it in the store a week ago, it reminded me of you." Even though I still hadn't heard from him at the time, I couldn't help but pick up the tie anyway in hopes I would be able to tell him this exact story.

This time the movement was deliberate. The slow whine of my hips put the perfect amount of torturous pressure against his groin. Each move made him harder, which meant he pressed into me more until the seat of my panties was not only soaked but deftly wedged against my clit. Our breaths were so in sync, I don't think we could have planned it any better if we'd tried.

"You've never even seen me in red." And it was clear by the way his words caught in his throat he was affected just as much as I was.

"True, but it caught my eye when I wasn't even looking for it. It was bold, wouldn't be ignored, and if you look closely—and I mean really look—you can see the intricate little designs you probably didn't notice before. It surprises you...makes you feel like it's just something you have to have. Sound familiar?"

I leaned down just enough so our foreheads touched as I picked up the pace, now outright grinding back and forth on the dick I wanted to feel inside me *so fucking bad.*

"Maybe. Are you saying I'm something you just have to have?" And as he asked the question, I felt his hips punch upwards, pulling a groan of my own from my throat.

Finally stopping my gyrations, I pressed my lips to his. "Not something. *Someone.*"

The kiss that followed held every bit of the hunger and longing I'd been holding for him for the last two weeks. When his tongue tangled with mine, I couldn't help but rotate my hips again, needing to feel the delicious friction the combination of his hardness against my lace had been giving me just a few moments before. It felt so *goddamn good*. Dry humping was a lost art, and *fuck* if this didn't show me we needed to bring that shit back.

"*Ahhh,*" I hissed against his lips as a shudder racked my body. I could come just like this. Just keep going until I fell apart right in his lap with his tongue tangled with mine and my nails digging into his chest before he ever even had a chance to slip inside me. It was tempting, especially when I opened my eyes to see him straining against the tie as if he were *desperate* to get his hands on me.

But I wasn't quite ready for that.

"Now..." I started as I pulled back. The way he lifted his head trying to follow made my nipples pebble and my stomach clench.

So goddamn needy.

"Are you sure you're not uncomfortable?"

This time when he answered, there was more confidence in his voice. "I'm fine. A little anxious, maybe."

"Anxious and uncomfortable or anxious and intrigued?"

Admittedly, I was a little surprised when Philip didn't roll his eyes at my question. Even if he had, I wouldn't have been bothered. I knew how important it was to gauge his comfort level. My goal for the night was to help him get out of his head and get his mind off of everything, but a big part of that was him being able to enjoy this experience.

Instead of appearing annoyed, I watched as Philip took a moment to think about his answer. His brows were knitted together in concentration as he turned my question over in his mind.

"Anxious...and intrigued."

As he said it, his shoulders relaxed and the tension his wrists had been placing on the knot started to loosen. "I promise."

"Good." I took a look at my handiwork. "Because now I feel confident in telling you that you won't be getting out of that any time soon. At least..." Dipping my hand between us, I slipped it into his briefs, taking hold of the very thing I'd just been driving wild. "Not until I'm ready for you to."

This time when he groaned, it sounded as if it'd come from deep within his chest. His tip was slick with precum and at that realization, I couldn't help but lick my lips. I remembered how he tasted and *shit*, I wanted it on my tongue again.

"It looks like you're already making a mess for me," I whispered as I slid back, traveling down until I was eye level with his briefs.

"Actually..." I cocked my head to the side. "I can't tell if that's your mess or mine," I giggled.

If I had to guess, I'd say it was both. His tip may have been dripping, but I knew the sticky mess coating my lips also had something to do with the wet spot I was currently looking at.

"What if I told you I wanted a taste?" I asked, my voice teasing as I pulled his briefs down little by little.

"Please," he groaned.

"Please what?"

"Pl-please taste it."

I smiled to myself, enjoying the sound of his begging as what I was looking for sprang into view. "Please taste it... who?"

Rubbing my cheek along the pretty, brown, veiny shaft, I swear I heard him stop breathing.

"Who, Philip? Be a good boy and tell me what I want to hear."

"Miss Raegyn," he moaned, and because now I was the one who was so goddamn eager, I didn't wait another second before I began to swallow his dick.

"*Fuck!*"

One desperate word was all it took for me to go into overdrive, licking along his shaft as if it were the same flavor as my favorite popsicle. Hell, it just might be. I couldn't get enough. What was meant to be a few teasing sucks quickly turned into a full-on mission to get more of the slightly salty flavor I'd begun to crave.

I wanted it.

Needed it.

Fuck the full five-star meal we had out in the kitchen, this was the only thing I wanted to feast on tonight. The combination of his taste, how he panted my name, and the not-so-subtle way his body tensed as I listened to him struggle against his restraints made for such a heady fucking experience. Dinner from my second-favorite restaurant couldn't even come close.

As one hand wrapped around the base of him, the other reached down even lower to cup his balls.

He stiffened with a curse and because this particular brand of torture was my favorite, I pulled him out of my throat and instead used my hand to stroke him from root to tip as I dipped my tongue lower and licked along his sack.

"Mi—*holy hell, Raegyn, please.*"

Why did the sound of his begging make my pussy so fucking wet?

"That's not my name."

"*Miss Raegyn.*" This time when he said it, I couldn't help but look up at him. There was no stopping the whimper that left me when I found him watching me as I sucked one ball into my mouth, then the other, causing his body to jerk as a whimper that matched my own left his lips. Watching as I moved back up until my tongue was swirling around his tip, lapping at the fresh spurts of precum that appeared, and sucking on it ever so lightly in a way that seemed to make his body clench and sag at the same time.

"You want to come, baby?" I asked in the sweetest voice I could muster.

He nodded in response and the gesture came so fast, I almost laughed.

"How bad?"

"*So fucking bad.*"

"But you know you can't come until I tell you to, right?"

"Yes." And it was clear it pained him to even say the word because he understood the truth of it.

"Good. Because as much as I would love for you to shoot that delicious ass treat down my throat...I have somewhere even better for it to go."

With his briefs left at his knees, I started to climb back up before he stopped me with a hurried "Wait!"

I paused, wondering if this was becoming too much for him. "Do you need to use the safeword, PJ?"

He shook his head immediately, which left me a bit confused.

"I wa-want to t-taste it." The hitch in his words was slightly distracting, or maybe that was because I knew they were in reaction to me. Since it was clear he wasn't ready to stop, I went back to giving his dick slow strokes.

"Taste..."

Letting his head fall back against the pillow, I watched as his chest heaved as he tried to catch his breath.

"If you want something from me, baby, the only way to get it is to ask like a good boy, remember?"

I felt his dick twitch at my words and couldn't help but smile. He loved when I called him that as much as I did.

"You said next time, I could taste it."

My pussy thumped once it dawned on me what he was referring to. "I'm pretty sure I said *maybe*, PJ. I don't know. Do you think you've earned it? You weren't exactly on your best behavior, remember." I paused, giving my wrist a twist, and his hips thrust up in reaction.

"But...maybe just this once. For incentive."

After swiping my thumb across his tip, I rose until my lower half was straddling his and slid that very same thumb across his bottom lip.

"Lick."

One word. One command. About one second before he did exactly as I said.

Holy shit.

His eyes closed as he savored the precum lingering on his tongue. While he was distracted, I wasted no time lifting up just enough to pull my panties to the side and slip his dick inside of me to wrap him in every inch of warmth my pussy had to offer. There was something so...*filthy* about fucking a man without getting completely undressed.

As I settled, taking time to get used to the painfully beautiful way he was stretching me, my eyes caught his. "Delicious, baby?"

"Not as delicious as you." And suddenly that cocky smile I'd missed so much appeared, causing me to give him one of my own.

"Oh, trust me, I know. But it's pretty damn close."

I started slow, my pace the perfect sort of torture. At first it was just to tease him, but *goddamn*, he was so fucking thick that I couldn't do anything but take my time. Even with how wet I was, he stretched me to the point of a slight burn, but it felt *so fucking good*. Better than I'd even imagined. By the time I'd taken all of him, I was so full I didn't even know if I'd be able to move.

But my mama didn't raise no punk and she certainly didn't raise a quitter.

I planted both hands on Philip's chest as I found my footing on either side of him, ready to take us both on the ride of our lives.

"I swear, Philip," I gasped as I rocked back and forth on my heels, putting everything I had into my movements, my head falling forward ever so slightly as a whine crept up my throat. "You're not playing fair."

He huffed as he watched me, lids lowered with desire, head falling to the side as he tried and failed to get loose to touch me. "I'm no—*shit*—not playing fair?"

"Not at all. Because if I had known the dick would be like this, *feel* like this, I swear I would've never let you disappear two weeks ago."

Fuck that. If I had known it would be like this, I would've let him bend me over the desk that night in his office and never looked back.

"I take it back. You do owe me an apology."

This time the sound he let out was somewhere between a moan and a laugh. "For what?"

I fell to my knees, needing more. With my forehead buried in his chest and my ass clapping as I bounced up and down relentlessly on his dick, I bit into his skin, needing something, *anything*, to keep me from crying out.

I heard the curse he let out and I wasn't sure if it was from pain or pleasure, but I didn't care either way. It mixed perfectly with my whines and the sound of him thrusting into my wetness over and over again.

"For keeping this beautiful, thick ass dick from me." The way he angled his hips made his pelvis hit just the right spot for me to grind my clit against him as we fucked each other. "Now say you're sorry."

I looked up at him just in time to see his eyes glaze over with pleasure as they rolled to the back of his head.

He was close, his thrusts becoming frantic as he took the lead. I wasn't ashamed to say I couldn't keep up, finally stopping my own movements and letting him fuck into me.

Talk about topping from the goddamn bottom.

"Say it," I snapped, my orgasm lurking just below the surface. By the way his dick was beginning to swell inside of me, I knew he wouldn't be too far behind.

"I'm...I'm sorry." His hands tried to grab hold of the tie to give him just a bit more leverage. "I'm so fucking sorry, Miss Raegyn."

"*Fuck, baby*...you better be."

Finding one last burst of strength, I leaned back up and put my hands against his chest. My hips rolled in time with his thrusts, both of us racing to the finish line.

"Now be a good boy and show me just how sorry you are." A sob escaped my lips. "Come for me."

He groaned, brows knitted in concentration. "Shit...

where?" he asked through gritted teeth. "Just tell me where!"

"The only place your cum belongs if it's not down my throat." I couldn't help but smile as I gasped. "Inside this sweet pussy."

Those four words were exactly what he needed to send him over the edge. His long, uninterrupted moan was music to my ears as my walls began to spasm at the feeling of each warm rope of cum coating them. The sensation triggered my own orgasm as my whine turned into a wail and my body began to tremble, more sensitive than I'd anticipated.

"Holy shit."

That was all I could say a few minutes later after we'd both finally come down and he wrapped his arms around me after I'd managed to find the strength to untie him.

"You can say that again."

"Oh, don't worry...I'm sure I will. Just as soon as I get this cat nap and let you fuck me again."

philip

"SO...I MAY HAVE LIED EARLIER."

Not exactly the words a man wanted to hear after a toe-curling orgasm...or three.

If I had the strength to do anything other than raise my fork to my mouth, she might have gotten a worried glance out of me, but as it was, I barely had the energy to eat.

My stamina was nothing to sneeze at. Some might call it impressive for my age. And yet after three rounds of the best sex of my life, I was literally spent. And that was with the couple hours of sleep I'd gotten in between each. I was pretty sure my dick couldn't even get hard right now if I wanted it to. But then I'd thought the same thing after our second round at three in the morning, yet when eight rolled around and I woke up to Raegyn's mouth wrapped around me, warm, wet, and ready to suck the soul and cum out of me, he showed me he had a little bit of life left in him.

"Okay, I'll bite if you chew." I raised the forkful of food to her lips this time as she rolled her eyes at my corny choice of words. Eggplant Parmesan may not be the most conventional breakfast, but it was a fucking delicious one.

"Cute."

"Not as cute as you."

"Of course not," she said in a tone that said 'tell me something I don't know.'

"Glad we're on the same page. Now, what's going on?" I paused, worried running through me. "Please don't tell me you lied about being on birth control." *If she had...she was most definitely pregnant after all the cum I'd—*

"Oh, hell no," she said, sounding exactly like one of the characters from the 2000s era Black sitcom she'd told me she loved. "That's definitely not it. This right here"—she gestured to her naked body, which was still partially covered by the sheet she'd brought to the floor with us—"is not a baby-making machine. Love the practice, but the actual implementation and execution can go straight to hell."

I let out a sigh of relief. "Good. One child is all I can handle right now and I can barely do that."

Understatement of the century.

"So glad you brought it up because that's actually what I want to talk to you about."

Moving the plate out of the way, she turned, elbow propped up on the floor as she stretched like an alley cat, the sheet slipping just enough to expose the top of her breasts. The way I licked my lips had little do with the food and more to do with the way she looked at that moment: freshly fucked and completely satisfied.

Huh. I guess my dick *could* get hard right now without me even trying.

I was barely aware of what she was saying until two names caught my attention.

"Wait...what was that?"

"*I said*, I meant it last night when I told you you didn't

owe me an apology, but I do think one is owed." She paused. "To Trinity and Arthur."

A wave of annoyance flowed through me. Was she fucking serious right now?

"You're joking, right? Please tell me you're joking, gorgeous. If so, we're going to have to work on your so-called sense of humor."

"Please tell *me* you're joking if you think you *don't* owe one." Raegyn shook her head as she sat up completely and leaned her back against the chaise at the foot of her bed.

"What exactly am I apologizing for? Catching my best friend and daughter in multiple goddamn lies, the biggest one being that they're fucking each other?"

"No, how about for talking to them the way you did? Shit, screw Arthur. You owe Trinity the biggest apology after the way you spoke to her and *about* her. That's your *daughter*, Philip."

"Exactly," I said incredulously. What part of this was she not understanding?

"Yeah, exactly! And yet not only did you talk to her like she was a child instead of a grown woman, you talked about and around her like she was some random person you were disgusted with. Quite honestly, if you were my father talking to me that way, I would've cussed your ass out a lot worse."

I just sat there, food and hard dick forgotten because I could not believe what I was hearing right now. How the hell was I the one who was lied to, yet I was in the wrong?

Did I regret some of the things I'd said that day? Of course, I did.

Was it slowly killing me Trinity hadn't called or texted me since and had missed two of our standing brunch dates? Of course, it was.

It was clear to me that maybe I'd acted out of turn and that was *before* her mother had called to lay into my ass. Wasn't hard to figure out they'd talked and she'd already gotten Trinity's side of the story.

Maybe it was immature of me to be holding onto this grudge the way I was, but when the fuck was someone going to recognize how I'd been done wrong in all of this?

The people I thought I could trust had turned out to be anything but. Was I just supposed to be okay with that? Shrug my shoulders, let it go, and just say everything was fine? Fuck that.

Raegyn shook her head when I asked her as much.

"Of course not. I'm not saying you didn't have a right to be pissed off. You had every right. You were blindsided and that's not okay, nor am I trying to minimize your feelings. What I'm telling you is just because you were hurt didn't give you the right to hurt them, especially not Trinity. You two are still building your relationship, so try and see it from her side. How the fuck is she supposed to tell the father she just met she's in a brand-new relationship and *surprise*, it's with one of his best friends? There's literally no right way to tell your father something like that. The prospect of even telling you her boyfriend was your age probably already scared the shit out of her."

She was right. I knew she was right, but my pride wouldn't let me say it out loud. "So I'm just supposed to give everyone in this situation a pass, huh?"

Leaning forward to take hold of my chin, Raegyn turned my head to face her.

"Did you hear me say that? 'Cause I'm pretty sure none of those words came out of my mouth. What I'm telling you is be upset, be hurt. No one can take that away from you. But while you're doing that, be sure to pull your head out of your ass too. If you heard anyone else talking to Trinity the way you did, or Arthur for that matter, you'd be ready to take their head off. You are too fucking old to be throwing tantrums like the one you threw in that house. Be a grown ass man and tell your friends how you fucking feel, and then make shit right with your daughter."

Still not ready to admit she was right, I shook my head. "Yeah, well...I'll take your second piece of advice under consideration, but the first is a hell no. Fuck those friends of mine. With friends like them, who needs enemies?"

Rolling her eyes, she stood, dropping the sheet completely as a buzzing sounded through the condo. Going over to the intercom on the wall that matched the one I'd seen by her front door, she pressed a button I was sure went to the security station at the front desk.

"Yeah, well, lucky for your stubborn, arrogant ass, I'm a woman of action."

A few moments went by as I watched her walk to the bathroom. I knew she couldn't be getting ready to shower because she'd done that while I'd been setting up our morning bedside feast. When she came out with her curly hair up in a clip and went straight to the dresser, pulling out a pair of underwear and a sports bra, I gave her a confused look. It only grew when her doorbell rang.

"What are you doing? Who's at the door?"

"*I* am getting dressed, and *that* would be your special guests arriving...though I'll admit they're like forty-five minutes early. But we'll adjust."

Special guests? No.

"You didn't. *Please* tell me you didn't."

She shrugged as she barely spared me a glance while searching through another drawer. "Okay, then I won't tell you. You can just answer the door and find out for yourself."

That in itself told me everything I needed to know. Scrambling to my feet, I nearly knocked the plates over.

"Raegyn, *what the fuck?*" I bellowed. "Have you lost your goddamn mind? I cannot fucking believe this. What gives you the right to—"

"First of all, watch your tone when you're talking to me," Raegyn snapped as she pulled on the pair of biker shorts she'd just grabbed.

"Last time I checked, we're not in scene, *Miss Raegyn.*" Irritation dripped off my every word. If she thought the moniker gave her the right to meddle in my personal business, she was sorely mistaken.

"No, but we are still in my home." She slammed the drawer shut and pushed past me to head back into the bathroom. "So I suggest you act like you have some goddamn sense and remember that before I put your Black ass out."

I followed right behind her, needing to understand what was going on. "What are they even doing here?" She'd only ever met Arthur, so this wasn't making any sense to me.

Instead of answering right away, she took her time under the guise of brushing her teeth, as if she needed to be completely focused on the simple task.

"Raegyn." I didn't snap at her or raise my voice this time, but the urgency was clear.

"I might have run into Arthur at my favorite restaurant the other day. Purely coincidental. I don't think he was searching for me or anything, it just sort of...happened."

"And what, you just casually decided to further make my life implode?"

"So fucking dramatic." She rolled her eyes. "No. I

wasn't going to say anything to him at all, but he came over to speak to me. He was worried about how you were doing since apparently, I wasn't the only person you've been avoiding for the past two weeks. I told him I hadn't talked to you, but I was thinking about reaching out because I missed you."

Do not let the fact that she missed you and your heart just stuttered at the thought distract you from the issue at hand.

"And then..."

"And then we got to talking. It turned out he was meeting your other two friends there and they gave me their contact information, just in case I heard from you. It's been two weeks, PJ, and they were fucking concerned."

She switched from brushing her teeth to washing her face, finally turning to me once she was done. "I honestly intended on minding my business, but once I made up my mind that I wanted to see you this week, I took a leap. I thought I'd have more time to talk to you about it before they showed up, but...well, we didn't really do much talking last night or this morning, did we?"

No, we didn't. And honestly, even if we had, I didn't know if I'd be any less upset than I was right now.

"Better to ask for forgiveness than permission," she said, giving me a pat on the cheek.

"And what if I decide to just leave and say fuck all of you?" Even as I said it, I knew it was pointless because if I was being honest with myself, I knew that wasn't an option.

"Then you'll have to deal with the consequences. You're an adult, Philip, and I'm not here to make you do a goddamn thing. I'm just trying to give you a helping hand because something tells me you're too damn stubborn to do it yourself. Think really hard about how much longer you want to hold onto this shit because if you let it, it might just ruin your life."

Raegyn made her way to the bedroom door as the doorbell went off again. Before she left the room, she turned one more time, clearly not finished.

"And while you're at it, remember there are people in your life who actually care about you. If you're lucky, I can be one of them. Either way, I'm going to let the way you just called yourself cussin' at me slide because I know you have a lot of shit going on. I can admit I probably overstepped a bit and for that, I'm going to apologize. But fix your fucking attitude. Take a minute, catch your breath, calm the fuck down and then bring your ass out here and talk to these damn men so I can shower and walk around naked after I come back from the gym."

Without another word, she left the room. I heard her open the door to let in the new "guests," something that sounded suspiciously like "don't fuck up my house" and then the door slamming as she made her exit.

Fuck.

Part of me wanted to say screw her just to be spiteful and petty. Overstepped wasn't even the word. Where did she get off sticking her nose in my business? I mean, obviously I wasn't about to reach out to anyone first, but shouldn't that have been my decision?

Too bad the other half of me really did want to screw her because *surprise, surprise*, apparently I liked it when she took charge both in and out of the bedroom.

She was right when she said I needed a push. Even though my fingers had been itching to reach out to literally any and everyone I had issues with, my pride held me back. What she did may have been an invasion of my privacy, but if I was being honest with myself, it was a much needed one. By taking the control out of my hands and placing it in her own, she'd still left me the choice to decide what I wanted to do while also giving me the means to do what I *needed* to do.

With my plan to spend the rest of the day polishing off the leftovers and spreading Raegyn across every surface of her condo clearly out the window—at least for now—it was time to do as she said and adjust.

I took my sweet time pulling on the sweats and t-shirt I'd grabbed from my overnight bag and handled whatever business I needed to in the bathroom. If they wanted to pop up on me, then they'd just have to deal with the fact that I wasn't in any particular rush to come out and see them face-to-face. Hopefully, at the very least, she'd left Arthur off this little impromptu guest list.

A man could dream, right?

TWELVE

philip

WHOEVER SAID *dreams do come true was a goddamn liar.*

After I'd stalled as much as I possibly could, I made my way out of the bedroom and down the hall to be greeted by not only Benjamin and Seth's faces, but Arthur's as well.

When Raegyn stuck her nose in something, she clearly stuck it all the way in. Just my luck.

Trying to appear unbothered, I brushed past them into the kitchen to grab a bottle of water. "I didn't peg any of you as stalkers, but I guess this is just more proof you can be something like friends for years and still not know each other, huh?" I took a sip from the bottle, hoping the cool drink would calm both my temper and my nerves.

Thanks to the open concept of her place, I could see all three of them clearly, even as Seth moved to take a seat in one of her living room chairs and Benji sat at the dining table. Arthur stood frozen in the space between the two areas, clearly unsure of where to put himself until he took a seat near Benji.

"Don't be a dick, Philip. We're not *something like friends*, we're actual friends," Benji scoffed.

"I'm just saying, could've fooled me. I wasn't aware friends treat each other the way you've treated me recently. Since when do friends lie? Keep secrets?" I turned my gaze toward Arthur, who could barely meet my eyes. "Sleep with each other's daughters? Sounds like strange friendship milestones to me."

"Right off into the deep end, huh? Thought we'd at least be able to start with pleasantries before we went to war," Benji said, clearly trying to make light of the uncomfortable situation.

"Funny for you to think that when we're dealing with Philip. I mean, how many times do I have to remind y'all to act like you actually know his ass for goodness' sake." Seth raised an eyebrow. "Even if you have been avoiding us and our phone calls like the plague."

"I thought being dramatic was supposed to be my area of expertise."

Had I been ignoring their phone calls and texts for the last two weeks? Yes.

Was it possible I'd gone as far as to instruct my staff not to let any of them near my office and to give away our reserved table since there was no way in hell I'd be letting them use it without me?

Again, yes.

Shit, maybe I really was the drama.

"Oh, you've still cornered the market on drama. I mean we figured you'd take a couple days to pout, but even Sage didn't think it'd last this long. I mean, Christ, if we hadn't run into Raegyn when we did, we'd be beating down your fucking door."

"Lucky me," I mumbled.

"Yeah, lucky you. How'd you manage to get her to put up with you anyway? She's way out of your league. I didn't think you stood a chance when we saw you walk up to her at the bar that night." A smirk appeared on Seth's face as he said the words.

"Always underestimating me, as if I'm not the most charming person you know."

"Uh, because you're not. My wife and girlfriend are."

I let out a snort as Benji laughed right along with me. It was so natural, falling back into this mode with them, but it didn't last long once I remembered why they were here.

"If you're finished insulting me, mind telling me what you're doing here?" I focused in on Arthur, who still hadn't said a word.

Between one minute and the next, the man of the hour let out a sigh. "Why do you think we're here, Philip? Because we're worried about you."

I couldn't help but scoff. "Worried about me or trying to do damage control because you got caught doing some bullshit?"

When he met my eyes, I tried not to let the raw emotion there get to me. "I can be honest and say it's a bit of both, at least for me. You've never gone radio silent like this before. It was a bit...off-putting."

"That's one word for it," Seth said, jumping in. "Ignoring *this* man, I get. But me and Benji? That's what I didn't see coming."

"You don't think you two deserved the silent treatment too, considering you knew about this shit all along?" I couldn't help but snap.

"Not all along," Benji interjected as he shook his head.

"We literally found out two weeks before you brought it up at the bar. This wasn't something we've all just been carrying around for months."

"Could've fooled me."

"Be serious for once, Philip."

"Oh, I'm dead ass serious right now. You really want me to believe this was all new information for the two of you? Okay, fine. Let's say it was. Is that supposed to change anything? You still kept this shit from me. Helped *him* keep it from me. Here I am, walking around telling you about how antsy I'm getting not knowing who the hell my daughter is spending her time with, and there you three are, listening to every word for however long. Not once did anyone open their goddamn mouth and say, 'Oh, by the way, Philip, no worries. That guy Trinity is seeing? He's right here!'"

I mean, for god's sake, did I have to spell out for them just how fucked up this situation really was?

We sat there, the three of us staring at one another in silence. What was probably only about three minutes felt like thirty.

"So the three of you are back to having nothing to say? That's just great."

Seth was the first to speak. "You're right." His words didn't just shock me, they apparently caught Benji and Arthur off guard too. "What? He is and you both know it, just like I do. And that's what you want to hear, right?" The last question was obviously directed at me.

That was what I wanted to hear...wasn't it?

I thought so, but now that I'd heard the words, I wasn't so sure. Suddenly, they weren't the only ones who were speechless.

Instead of saying anything, I pulled out a chair and took

a seat at the table while Seth left his own seat and came to join us, taking up the space in front of the counter that I'd just vacated.

"Want to hear the funny part?" I finally asked. "The thing that gets me more than anything is that it feels like this is just the beginning of you three casting me to the side and leaving me out of things."

And there it was. The truth of it all. Let's be honest, while I was upset about Arthur and Trinity being a couple, I knew that was just the surface issue. It was still mind-boggling, but the more I thought about it—and believe me, I'd thought about it a lot more than I cared to admit—the thing that hurt the most was feeling like I was losing my friends. Like they had this life and this world that they didn't want me to be a part of.

"I thought we were better than that. That when big shit happened in your lives, you'd include me. Yet one of the biggest things to happen to Arthur since Laura passed away occurs and no one even made an attempt to clue me in, even though it literally involves my family. Do you have any idea how that shit makes me feel? It's bad enough it always feels like none of you really take me seriously in the first place. This just felt like confirmation that I'm the odd man out in this group."

"Shit, man..." Benji leaned forward to put his hand on my shoulder. "I swear we didn't even think of it like that. We just...no one knew what the hell to say."

"How can you even think that? As if you weren't there when I married Melinda? Like Benji didn't include you in the conversation about moving in with Sage, or me coming to you to help me surprise the girls with that trip to Bali last year? You were the first person Arthur called after Laura's accident. We all share practically every important milestone with each other and have for years."

"And yet and still, you do nothing but roll your eyes when I talk sometimes. There are times when I call one of you to find out that you're all out on a group date together, or you make plans and don't think to invite me until it's an afterthought."

"Because we know you, Philip, and there's just certain shit you're not going to do and enjoy. And yeah, okay, we could ask, but we learned a long time ago that when it comes to date night activities, inviting you and your latest fling doesn't always go well. Hell, you're the one pointing out half the time how seriously you take bachelorhood and how very unserious you are about certain group situations. You don't even take yourself seriously half the time, but you're upset with us because we follow your lead? Do you hear how that sounds?"

Maybe a bit ridiculous, but then weren't all insecurities that way?

"Since it's obvious you need to hear at least one of us say it," Arthur started, "let me be clear when I say you've never been on the outs."

"So we're just going to act like I don't know what you say behind my back?"

"Behind your back? The only thing we say is the exact same thing we say to your face. You're a pompous, arrogant asshole who's a pain in the ass, but we wouldn't trade you for anybody."

Benji said it so matter-of-factly that it caught me off guard. "Don't act like you don't get sick of me."

"Of course, we get sick of you! Hell, I get sick of my damn self. Do you know how many times Sage has put this handsome bastard out since they moved in together just because the sound of his breathing gets on her nerves? Or how often Melinda and Alaina tell me they're sick of looking at my face? Arthur hung up on me literally a week ago because I was chewing too loudly in his goddamn ear—as if he doesn't literally chew like a cow."

"Hey!" Arthur said, and I had to stifle my laugh as Seth continued.

"Not to mention, how long have we all been friends? Decades at this point. I'd be more worried if we didn't want to choke the hell out of each other occasionally. Let's just lay it on the table, okay? We're all irritating as hell, and yes, sometimes you're more annoying than the rest of us, but so what? We already know that about you, Philip, just like we know you love the attention. Tell me I'm lying."

I couldn't exactly deny what he was saying.

"Exactly. It doesn't make us think less of you, and if you really thought it did, then maybe we've got even bigger problems than I thought."

He had me there. Honestly, it wasn't until I knew I was left out that I realized how much it bothered me when it happened. But each time, I just brushed it to the side because he was right. I didn't want to bring my latest fling to every little group outing and I certainly didn't really mind missing out on some of the things they did together. But this latest incident with Arthur and Trinity just sent me over an edge I hadn't even realized I was near.

I wasn't making this up. It did feel like sometimes they just preferred to be without me, but how would they know that if I didn't vocalize it? How would they know that while yes, I loved to tell a joke, that didn't mean I wanted to be the butt of them on a regular basis anymore?

Maybe...maybe I was ready to be a bit more serious and act my age. It wasn't the end of the world, right? I wanted my daughter to be able to trust me and my friends to confide in me. To give them the chance to be a bit more serious about me. But first, I would have to get serious about myself.

It was time for me to do exactly what Raegyn said and grow the hell up. God...maybe it was time to get a therapist. I clearly had some shit I needed to work out.

"You're a pain in the ass, Philip," Benji sighed. "And you're most certainly an asshole, but you're our asshole."

There was no stopping the chuckle that left me at hearing that because he was right—I was absolutely an asshole. It was one of my favorite qualities about myself.

The problem was, sometimes I got the nagging feeling that they were just...over my shit. Would there come a point where they were tired of putting up with me and cut me out completely? My life would be lonely as hell if I lost the people around me. The thought of being alone, without anyone to turn to, scared the shit out of me.

Damn...greatest fear unlocked, huh? Yeah, it was definitely time to find a therapist.

"I just— I know my extraordinary personality can be a bit much, so the thought that I'm going to be the one voted off the island just...gets to me sometimes."

"And the fact that you had no clue what the hell was going on just sort of solidified that for you," Benji finished as he nodded in understanding.

"Well, lucky for you, no one is getting voted off this island. At least not ours. Now, whatever island Raegyn is on? Yeah, I can't guarantee you'll get to stay on that one. She looked pissed when she left out of here," Seth snickered.

There was no real malice in my words when I shot a "fuck you" in his direction.

"Seriously, though, we're sorry. I feel like shit knowing that you've been carrying that insecurity around and everything that's happened only added to it. You don't have to keep that kind of shit in. None of us want that for you."

I nodded, both hearing and understanding what he was telling me.

"And trust me when I say, we've been telling this asshole since we found out that he needed to let you know what was going on." Benji shot Arthur a look and he had the decency to look somewhat embarrassed.

"He's right, they did. Relentlessly."

"And you didn't because..."

"Because how the hell am I supposed to look one of my best friends in the eye and tell him that I'm in love with the daughter he just met?"

"I don't know, maybe just like that."

There was no doubt in my mind I still would've been pissed off, but I would've gotten over it after a day or two. It certainly wouldn't have taken me two weeks to pull my head out of my ass, that's for sure.

Arthur dipped his head. "You have a point, I guess. It was just...hard. I haven't felt this way about anyone since Laura. Didn't think I was capable of feeling this way about someone else, honestly. It terrified the hell out of me that telling you could be the one thing that ended this relationship."

"End the relationship?" I asked, confused.

"Honestly, Philip, do you really think Trinity and I would've kept seeing each other if you truly didn't approve?"

I didn't even hesitate with my answer and neither did Benji and Seth. "Yes."

The fact that all three of us agreed sent us into a round of laughter that even Arthur had to join in on.

"Okay, so we probably would have, but it still would've devastated us both and we definitely would've slowed down a bit. You're important to me. Important to her. Neither one of us wants to lose you over this, no matter how much we love one another."

I let his words sink in. Did I really want to stand in the way of my best friend's happiness? Hell, did I want to stand in the way of my daughter's happiness? The answer was an obvious no. I was an asshole, but even I had my limits.

"You're really in love with her?"

His answer was clear when he looked me dead in the eyes and said, "I want to marry her."

Well, shit.

It didn't matter that I didn't have a response right away because while I sat speechless, he stood, digging into his pocket, and placed a small box on the table.

"You bought her a fucking ring?" exclaimed Seth.

Okay, so at least I wasn't the only one in shock right now.

"Yep."

"It's been three months."

"Closer to four at this point, but when you know, you know. It may sound unbelievable, but I want to spend the rest of my life with her if she'll let me."

I picked up the box, opening it to see one of the most stunning rings I'd ever laid eyes on inside. I always knew Arthur had great taste and there was no doubt in my mind that Trinity would love it.

"Well...there's only one thing left to say then." My eyes met his as I stood. "If you thought I was a major pain in the ass before, just wait until you have to start calling me dad."

The tension left his shoulders as we pulled each other in for a hug. As strange as it sounded, I couldn't think of anyone else who I'd trust Trinity with more. Her heart would be in good hands.

"You're going to be absolutely insufferable now aren't you?" asked Benji.

"Abso-fucking-lutely."

THIRTEEN

I COULDN'T STOP STARING at the ring sitting on Trinity's finger. It was...breathtaking. Honestly, Philip's description of it after he'd spilled the beans hadn't done it a lick of justice.

When I came back from the gym that day, I'd half-expected my place to be a mess. I just knew Philip was going to show his ass and I was going to regret sticking my nose where it didn't belong.

Imagine my surprise when instead of chaos, I walked in to find them watching SportsCenter while they ate up the rest of our leftovers. Didn't even have the decency to save me any—though apparently Philip hadn't gotten his fill because as soon as he'd ushered his friends out, he hoisted me up onto my kitchen counter and ate my pussy until I was in literal tears.

That was one way to say thank you.

Bringing myself back to the present, my eyes scanned the table before once again falling on Trinity's engagement ring. At least it gave me something to look at while we sat here in the most awkward ass silence I'd ever encountered.

If I had known the tension was going to be this thick between Trinity and her father, I would've kept my ass at home.

"Congratulations again, Trinity," I said, making an attempt to break the ice.

"Thanks," she said, giving me a soft smile before going back to picking at her cake. Philip had gotten a two-layer lemon cake to help celebrate the engagement in hopes it would soften her up a bit. It didn't exactly seem to be working.

We were at Philip's house on his covered porch, taking advantage of what had been a relatively nice day. After they'd cleared the air, Philip and Arthur both agreed he needed to sit down with Trinity and have a discussion, but apparently she was just as stubborn as her dad was because it had taken her another week to agree. They'd settled on a Sunday, hoping it would offer a bit of reprieve since he usually left the day reserved for her anyway. I'd initially thought it should just be the three of them, but Philip said Arthur was adamant about me being there too—probably so he wouldn't have to suffer through the awkwardness alone.

After another five minutes of silence, Arthur finally spoke up. "For the love of God, one of you say something."

"I'm sorry."

Though I'd heard the words before, they still sounded foreign coming out of Philip's mouth. Even I knew he wasn't a man who apologized often.

Instead of responding, Trinity just crossed her arms over her chest and continued to watch him, waiting for whatever it was he was going to say next.

"The way I spoke to you that day, Trini...there's no

excuse. No matter how shocked or angry I was, I didn't have the right to speak to you or about you in that way."

"You're right. You didn't."

Philip bowed his head. "Well, you'll be happy to know Raegyn and Arthur both tore me a new one for it." Apparently, in addition to what Arthur had said to him in the foyer the day we caught them, he'd also had plenty to say at my condo before he left.

"Is this the part where I'm supposed to feel sorry for you?" she asked, and he cringed in response.

"Trinity," Arthur whispered, wrapping his arm around her shoulder. He seemed to be saying something else in her ear we couldn't hear. Whatever it was did the trick because she slowly let her arms down, and I could've sworn her eyes began to water.

"You hurt me." Her words were just below a whisper, but we could hear them all the same. "And honestly, I didn't expect you to be able to hurt me like that, which made it even worse."

Philip cursed under his breath as she continued.

"And I'm sorry, daddy. I'm sorry I lied to you and kept this from you, but you weren't supposed to react that way. You weren't supposed to be angry and yell and throw punches." I watched as she went to wipe away one of the tears that had begun to fall. Shit, if she started crying, then I was going to cry too, and I did not want *that* to happen.

She gave a weak laugh. "I mean okay, I did imagine it as the worst-case scenario, but I was really hoping you'd shock me and it wouldn't actually come down to you doing those things."

"And that's what makes it so much worse. You're right. Me losing my shit was absolutely the worst-case scenario and I wish I could take it back." He stood up, making his way to the other side of the table and stooping down so he was looking directly into her eyes.

"I'm not perfect."

"Talk about an understatement," I said, and Trinity burst into a laugh right along with me.

"If the peanut gallery is finished..." he said, shooting me a look. I threw up my hands, signaling for him to continue.

"Like I was saying, as my new therapist pointed out to me I'm not perfect. And despite my best efforts, I probably never will be. Oh, and apparently I have some underlying abandonment issues I need to work on. Go figure." Trinity's eyes widened as if the revelation that her father would actually go and talk to someone was something she hadn't considered.

"But what I can try to be is better. I'm still figuring this fatherhood thing out. Hell, I'm still figuring out this whole 'how to be a mature adult' thing too if we're being honest. It's going to take a lot of practice and a hell of a lot of patience."

I watched as Philip reached out his hand and felt my heart squeeze when Trinity took it into hers. "But I hope you know I mean it when I say I'm trying my hardest to get this shit right more often than not."

His eyes flickered over to Arthur, who was watching them with a small smile on his face.

"And if this old asshole is who you want to spend the rest of your life with, well then...who am I to stop you?"

There were about thirty seconds between his last words and Trinity throwing her arms around his neck to pull him in for a hug he gladly returned. Shit, now my tears really were threatening to spill over.

"Do you really mean it?"

"I do. Of course, I do. Would I have helped your hopeless ass fiancé pick out that ring if I didn't?"

"Philip," I hissed, and the only thing he could do was laugh.

"Okay, so maybe he picked it out himself, but I *did* give him my blessing last week so that has to count for something," he said as they pulled away from one another.

Trinity beamed. "And it does, I promise."

"Good. Now I need you to promise me something else while you're at it."

She lifted her eyebrows curiously, and even I leaned forward a bit 'cause there was no telling what was about to come out of this man's mouth.

"You promise not to keep anything else from me and I'll promise to take it easy on my future son-in-law. Or at least keep the difficulty level as low as possible."

Trinity groaned as she rolled her eyes while I shook my head and Philip took his seat next to me.

"You're ridiculous, you know that?" I said.

"Ridiculous is awfully close to the word 'genius,' so I'll allow it."

"Raegyn, how exactly have you been putting up with him? Are you sure this is what you want to do? We can find you an escape route. Just say the word."

I laughed at Arthur, letting out a small yelp as Philip pulled me into his lap.

"Try it and I'll snatch my blessing right back, Artie boy. Don't test me. You've got your own girl, so leave mine alone."

"Who said I was yours at all?" I teased, wrapping my arms around his neck as his fingers found their way up the bottom of my shirt until they traced along my skin.

"I did."

"Mmhmm, and who exactly are you to make decisions about anything? I'm in charge, remember?"

"Oh, I remember...and I'm hoping for another lesson as soon as these two clear out."

"Ewww, dad, please!" Trinity squealed as she covered her ears and buried her face in Arthur's arm.

"Don't *ewww* me. We're all grown here, remember? Or did you forget I found you standing in Arthur's kitchen with nothing but a shirt on?"

She groaned, and I couldn't help but giggle as Philip nuzzled my collarbone. "Ain't much fun when the rabbit got the gun, is it?"

It might not have been fun for them, but me? I planned on having my favorite type of fun as soon as this cute little get-together was over, just as he'd suggested.

I couldn't wait because if Philip was right about one thing, it was that both of our lives were better when I was the one in control.

a final word

This is it! Thank you for reading Sweet Control, the fourth and final book in the Sugared and Spiced series. I know Philip has been getting on y'all nerves since the beginning but as promised, he finally got his just desserts. He and Raegyn were such a great time and I hope you enjoyed them as much as I have.

If you're able, please find the time to leave a rating and/or review on your favorite platform (Goodreads, Storygraph, etc.). They're the best way to help readers find new favorites and so important when supporting indie authors.

To keep up-to-date on upcoming Lady Marie projects, be sure to sign up for the Spice In Your Life Newsletter, join me on Patreon (Lady Marie Affair), check out my linktree, and follow me on social media @ladymariewrites.

To order a signed copy of any of my paperback projects, merch, or web exclusives, please visit the Lady Marie Shop at www.payhip.com/ladymariewrites

acknowledgments

Special thank you to my Patreon members. You took this ride with me for my first Patreon serial and your enthusiasm kept me going. I can't wait to see what we get into next.

You all already know I have a team behind me that is unmatched. People who are in my corner no matter what and are always there when I need them. Love y'all!

And finally, I really want to thank the readers. Y'all truly keep me going even when I'm not sure that I can. You're supportive, patient, and believe in me even when I don't believe in myself. The way y'all eat these stories up is amazing and I'll never be able to thank y'all enough. As long as you've got me, I've got you.

also by lady marie

SISTERS & SERENDIPITY SERIES

Worth It (A Fake Dating Novel)

Found Forever (An Established Couple, After the HEA Novella)

SUGARED AND SPICED SERIES

Sugar, Sugar (An Age Gap, Sugar Arrangement Novella)

Sweet Heat (A FFM Age Gap, Sugar Arrangement Novella)

Sugar-Coated Kisses (An Age Gap Insta-love Novella)

Sweet Control (An Age Gap, Sugar Arrangement Novella)

SLEIGH THE NIGHT COLLECTION

After Tonight (A Brother's Best Friend Novella, *Sleigh the Night* Prequel)

Sleigh the Night (A Winter Shorts Collection)

HOLIDAY NOVELLAS AND SHORT STORIES

With Sugar on Top (A Sugared and Spiced NYE Short)

Sinnamon & Golds (A Lick Back Season, Thanksgiving Novella)

Szn's Greetings (A Sinnamon & Golds Christmas Short)

Resolutions (A New Year's Novellette)

www.ingramcontent.com/pod-product-compliance
Lightning Source LLC
Chambersburg PA
CBHW022035170626
46808CB00003B/1212